THE SECRET OF PIRATES' HILL

The HARDY BOYS *Mystery Stories*
BY FRANKLIN W. DIXON

The Tower Treasure
The House on the Cliff
The Secret of the Old Mill
The Missing Chums
Hunting for Hidden Gold
The Shore Road Mystery
The Secret of the Caves
The Mystery of Cabin Island
The Great Airport Mystery
What Happened at Midnight
While the Clock Ticked
Footprints under the Window
The Mark on the Door
The Hidden Harbor Mystery
The Sinister Sign Post
A Figure in Hiding
The Secret Warning
The Twisted Claw
The Disappearing Floor

The Mystery of the Flying Express
The Clue of the Broken Blade
The Flickering Torch Mystery
The Melted Coins
The Short-Wave Mystery
The Secret Panel
The Phantom Freighter
The Secret of Skull Mountain
The Sign of the Crooked Arrow
The Secret of the Lost Tunnel
The Wailing Siren Mystery
The Secret of Wildcat Swamp
The Crisscross Shadow
The Yellow Feather Mystery
The Hooded Hawk Mystery
The Clue in the Embers
The Secret of Pirates' Hill
The Ghost at Skeleton Rock
The Mystery at Devil's Paw

The Mystery of the Chinese Junk

The cannon ball missed the boys by inches!

THE SECRET
OF PIRATES'
HILL

BY

FRANKLIN W. DIXON

NEW YORK
GROSSET & DUNLAP
Publishers

CONTENTS

CHAPTER		PAGE
I	UNDERWATER DANGER	1
II	A SUSPICIOUS CLIENT	11
III	A MOTORCYCLE CLUE	19
IV	NEW TACTICS	27
V	THE STAKEOUT	35
VI	PROFITABLE SLEUTHING	44
VII	MYSTERIOUS ATTACKERS	51
VIII	THE BATTLE OF BAYPORT	59
IX	PIRATES' HILL	68
X	A SPY	76
XI	STRANGE FOOTPRINTS	83
XII	A FRIENDLY SUSPECT	92
XIII	OVERBOARD!	99
XIV	THE ELUSIVE MR. X	107
XV	AN ALIAS	117
XVI	A SURPRISING SEARCH	127
XVII	A MISSING PAL	134
XVIII	MIXED IDENTITIES	142
XIX	CHET'S KIDNAP STORY	150
XX	AN IMPOSTOR	158
XXI	THE WRECK	168
XXII	GUNNER'S TOOLS	175
XXIII	GUARDING A DISCOVERY	183
XXIV	HUMAN TARGETS	192
XXV	DIVERS' REWARD	203

THE SECRET OF PIRATES' HILL

CHAPTER I

Underwater Danger

"DON'T forget, Frank, any treasure we find will be divided fifty-fifty!" Blond, seventeen-year-old Joe Hardy grinned. He checked his skin-diving gear and slid, flippers first, over the gunwale of their motorboat.

"I'll settle for a pot of gold," retorted Frank.

He was similarly attired in trunks, air tank, and face mask, and carried a shark knife. The brothers had anchored their boat, the *Sleuth,* off a secluded area of beach. It ran beneath a low, sand-dune-covered, rocky promontory called Pirates' Hill. The only other boat in sight was that of an old fisherman out for an early-morning catch.

"Here goes!" said Frank as he plunged into the cool waters of the Atlantic. Together, the boys swam toward the bottom.

Suddenly Joe clutched his brother's arm and

1

pointed. Twenty feet in front of them and only a short distance from the surface was another skin diver in a black rubber suit and a yellow-trimmed cap. The barbed shaft of a spear gun he held was aimed in their direction!

As the man pulled the trigger, Joe gave his brother a hard shove, separating the boys. The arrow flashed between them and drifted away.

"Wow, what's that guy trying to do?" thought Frank. Had he mistaken them for fish? Or was he just practicing?

The diver made no attempt to come forward and explain or apologize. Instead, he swam off.

"That's strange," Joe said to himself.

Motioning for his brother to follow, he swam toward the diver to find out what he was doing. But the spearman, with powerful strokes, shot to the surface. Apparently he did not want to be questioned.

Pointing, Joe indicated to Frank, "Up and after him!"

As the brothers popped above the waves, they looked about. The *Sleuth* lay twenty feet away and the old fisherman was still in the same spot. But the spearman was nowhere in sight.

Frank and Joe lifted their face masks. "Where did he go?" Frank called.

"I can't figure it out," Joe replied, treading water and gazing in all directions. "Let's ask that fisherman."

The diver deliberately aimed his spear gun at the boys

The boys swam to their motorboat and hung on to the gunwales. Frank called out, "Ahoy there! Did you see another skin diver around here?"

"What say?" The old fellow, who was wearing a cap which shaded most of his wrinkled face, appeared to be deaf.

Frank shouted, "Did you see a skin diver wearing a black outfit?"

The man laid his pole in the bottom of the boat and cupped both hands over his ears. "Who had a fit?" he called.

"Never mind!" Joe shouted. With a wink at his brother, he said, "Guess he didn't see anybody."

Conjecturing that the stranger might have swum slightly beneath the surface and taken off toward shore, Frank and Joe decided to resume their diving.

"Down we go," Joe said, as he readjusted the straps that held the air tank on his back. "But keep your eyes open for that spearman."

"Right."

Again the boys submerged. There was no sign of the other diver.

"He sure got away from here fast," Frank said. "I'd like to know who he is and what he thought he was doing!"

Long, strong strokes with their rubber-finned legs forced the boys downward through seaweed gardens. Small fish swished in and out among

the fronds. Seeing no interesting objects to sal-
vage, Frank signaled Joe to head for deeper water.
Air bubbles rippled steadily upward.

Suddenly a giant form appeared before Frank.
A black shark? Frank unsheathed his knife and
faced the huge fish. Just then the monster
swerved and Frank got a better look at it.

"A tuna!" he told himself, relieved.

The fish swam close. The noses of boy and
fish nearly touched. Frank chuckled at the droopy
expression in the tuna's eyes.

As Frank turned to see if his brother was
watching, he felt a sudden jar and his face mask
was nearly ripped off. Frank clawed desperately
to put it in place. "What's going on?" he thought
as unconsciousness swept over him.

Joe, who had seen the whole episode, was hor-
ror-struck. Another shaft from a spear gun had
zipped through the murky deep. From the vast
number of bubbles rising through the water, Joe
realized that his brother's air hose had been
pierced. Water was flooding in!

With powerful strokes, he reached Frank's side.
Towing the limp form with one hand, Joe headed
for the *Sleuth's* anchor line, dim in the distance.
Working his fins as violently as possible, he
fought his way toward it for what seemed an
eternity.

Finally Joe reached the rope and pulled himself surfaceward. When both boys bobbed into

the air again, Joe tore off Frank's headgear, holding his face above the waves. Then he pushed his brother inside the boat and scrambled after him.

"Frank!" Joe cried out, laying his brother in a prone position and feverishly applying artificial respiration.

Minutes passed before Frank stirred. Joe continued his treatment until he heard a moan, then a feeble question.

"Ugh—where—what happened?"

"We were shot at again and you were hit!" Joe said, helping his brother sit up. "This time it was deliberate."

"The same diver?"

"It must have been."

"Probably hiding behind an underwater rock," Frank concluded.

At that moment the boys heard the fisherman call out, "Something wrong over there?"

Joe shook his head and the old fellow continued his fishing.

"That devilish skin diver must be a phantom," Frank said, after filling his lungs with deep drafts of air.

"I still can't figure him out," Joe mused. "Say, do you suppose he's looking for sunken treasure and wanted to keep us away?"

"I never heard anybody talk about sunken treasure off Bayport," Frank said.

"No," Joe agreed. "Well, pal, I think you've had enough for one morning. Let's go home."

Waving at the fisherman, he pulled up anchor and started the motor. Two miles away on Barmet Bay was the boathouse where the boys kept the *Sleuth*. As they turned toward the bay entrance, Joe grinned ruefully. "I wish we could have kept that spear for a clue," he remarked, "but it passed clean through your air hose and disappeared."

"Better luck next time."

"What!" Joe exclaimed. "Better no next time at all!" Then he said, "We wouldn't know that fellow even if we should meet him again."

"I did notice one thing," said Frank. "He had a yellow band around that black swim cap he wore."

"Pretty slim clue. You feeling okay, Frank?" Joe asked, observing how pale his brother was.

The older boy said he had fully recovered from the shock. "Say, look!" he added a few minutes later. "Someone's waiting for us at the dock."

Drawing closer, they saw that the man was about thirty-five years old, stockily built, and had wiry, black hair. He stood motionless, his legs braced apart, looking intently at the approaching boys. Joe ran the *Sleuth* inside the boathouse and the brothers stepped ashore.

"Good morning," the stranger said. "My name's Clyde Bowden. I'm from Tampa, Florida. I assume you're the Hardys?"

"That's right," Frank replied, as the trio exchanged handshakes. "What can we do for you?"

"A detecting job."

"That's for us!" said Joe excitedly, but Frank added cautiously, "Let's hear about it first."

The Hardys, star athletes at Bayport High, were the sons of Fenton Hardy. Once a crack detective with the New York City Police Department, Mr. Hardy was now an internationally famous private sleuth. The brothers often helped their father on cases and also had solved many mysteries of their own.

Their first big success was *The Tower Treasure,* and only recently they had had a hair-raising adventure in tracking down *The Clue in the Embers.* Now they seemed to be headed for another mystery.

"How did you know where to find us?" Joe asked.

"I just left your home on Elm Street," Bowden replied. "Learned from your mother I might meet you here. I understand you're amateur sleuths."

"Yes," said Frank. "While we stow our diving gear and get into some clothes, suppose you tell us about your case."

The boys put their skin-diving equipment in

a locker of the *Sleuth,* then pulled on shirts, dungarees, and sneakers.

"I hear that you fellows, as well as your father, do a pretty clever job of detecting," Bowden began.

"Mother didn't tell you that," said Frank, smiling. "She never brags about us."

"No. As a matter of fact, I heard it from your postman. I asked him which house you lived in." Bowden chuckled. "He gave me a five-minute talk about all the cases you've solved. He seemed a bit disappointed that I was going to ask you in person to take on a case, instead of sending a mysterious-looking letter that he could deliver!"

Frank and Joe grinned at each other as the three left the boathouse, then listened intently as Bowden explained the case. He was searching for an early eighteenth-century cannon known as a Spanish demiculverin. It was supposed to be in the vicinity of Bayport.

"A Spanish cannon in Bayport?" Joe asked unbelievingly.

"I have reliable information it's around here," Bowden answered. "Although I'm not in a position to tell you how I know about the cannon, I'm certain that with your assistance I can locate it."

As they walked toward the Hardy home, Frank asked the man for the dimensions of the cannon. Bowden described it as being nine feet long and weighing 3,200 pounds. "It fires an eight-pound shot," he added.

"What do you want the old cannon for?" Joe asked.

Bowden smiled, somewhat embarrassed. "Believe it or not, I'm helping to outfit the pirate boats to be used in the famous Gasparilla Exposition in Tampa this year," he replied. "All the details, including the guns, must be authentic."

"That's very interesting," said Frank, as they turned a corner toward the town square. "I should think that the type of cannon you're looking for would be found somewhere around the Caribbean rather than this far north. I've read that many Spanish ships were wrecked—"

Frank stopped speaking as a deafening boom suddenly shook the air.

"What was that?" Bowden gasped, paling.

"It came from the square," Frank replied. "Sounds like trouble. Come on. Let's find out what happened!"

CHAPTER II

A Suspicious Client

WITH Bowden trailing behind, Frank and Joe sprinted toward a crowd of people milling in the town square. They were gathered around an old Civil War mortar that stood on a pedestal. White powder smoke drifted from the muzzle.

"Somebody fired the old gun!" Joe cried out in astonishment. "Do you smell that powder?"

"It must have been an accident," Frank said.

As the brothers shouldered their way through the crowd they saw Officers Smuff and Riley of the local police force being besieged with questions from the onlookers.

"What happened?"

"Who set it off?"

"Was anyone hurt?"

Before the policemen could reply, a booming voice sounded above the babble and a grizzled old man, dressed in a Minute Man's outfit, complete to tricorn hat and leggings, strode up beside the mortar.

"I cain't understand what all this here fussin' is about," he drawled.

At this, Officer Riley drew himself erect and demanded, "And who do you think you are in that rig?"

The old man smiled and his weather-beaten face creased into long lines. He told Officer Riley that he was Jim Tilton, a retired artillery sergeant of the National Guard. He had been asked by Police Chief Collig to take charge of the Independence Day cannon salute. "An' I think I look 'propriate for this job," he added.

"But this ain't the Fourth!" Riley protested. "It's only the first. Why should you come around here bombardin' the town without warnin'?"

The old-timer raised his hands good-naturedly. "I'm mighty sorry I caused so much fuss. After all, I wasn't usin' a ball. I just had some powder an' waddin' in her."

Tilton pulled a letter from his pocket and showed it to the officers. It was from Chief Collig and the Fourth-of-July Committee, granting permission for Tilton to test the mortar.

"Well, there was no harm done," Riley said, "but I should have been notified. But anyway, we know the gun is ready—we and everybody for five miles around!"

Reassured, the crowd dispersed as Officers Smuff

and Riley herded them off. Sergeant Tilton remained near the mortar, talking with a few men. The Hardys moved closer to get a better look at the old sergeant and the equipment he had been using.

Bowden also edged forward and stared with keen interest at the various markings on the gun. He told the boys that this was a Federal piece.

"It was cast at the same arsenal that turned out the famous 'Dictator,'" he said. "That was a thirteen-inch mortar used against Petersburg, Virginia, in the Civil War."

Tilton raised his eyebrows in surprise. "Land sakes," he remarked, "you know a lot! An' here I am, a veteran of that famous battle between the *Monitor* an' the *Merrimac,* an' I didn't never suspect anything like that about this ol' hunk o' iron."

Everyone laughed and Joe quickly calculated that for Tilton's tall tale to be true he would have to be well over a hundred years old.

As the sergeant began to clean the barrel of the old weapon, Bowden turned to Frank and Joe. "My offer to you," he said in a low voice, "is one thousand dollars if you find the Spanish cannon."

Frank and Joe were amazed. A thousand dollars for an old gun to be used in a pageant!

Sensing their thoughts, Bowden quickly added, "I'm a man of means and can well afford it."

He explained that he had already combed

Bayport proper. The boys' responsibility would lie in searching the surrounding areas and nearby towns. Bowden said he was staying at the Garden Gate Motel on the state highway and could be reached there if anything developed.

"We don't charge for our sleuthing," Frank informed the man.

Bowden was astonished. "You've solved all your cases for nothing?"

Joe nodded. "If we should help you," he said, "it will be on that basis."

"Okay. But believe me, I'll make it worth your while somehow!" Then, seeing that Tilton was preparing to leave, Bowden hastily excused himself. "I have a few questions to ask this old codger. See you later."

"Okay, Mr. Bowden," Frank replied. "We'll think about your request and let you know our decision."

The Hardys crossed the square and headed for the police station to report the underwater attack on them. They went directly to Chief Collig, a solidly built man in his late forties. He often co-operated with the Hardys on their cases, and now listened intently to their latest adventure.

"This is serious," he said. "I'll notify the harbor patrol to be on the lookout for a skin diver wearing a black suit and a swim cap with a yellow stripe around it."

The boys thanked him and left. As they walked

up Elm Street on which they lived, their conversation turned to Bowden.

"It seems that we're back in business!" Joe remarked. "Let's take on the case."

"I'm a little worried about it," Frank replied. "The whole setup seems a bit phony."

"You're imagining things, Frank. Bowden's a nice fellow."

Joe was naturally impulsive and always ready for action. Frank reminded him of the many times they had met people who had seemed to be aboveboard yet had turned out to be dishonest.

"But we'd still have fun looking for the cannon," Joe insisted. "What could we lose?"

"Nothing, maybe."

At the rambling stone house in which they lived, the boys were greeted by their petite mother and their tall, angular Aunt Gertrude. She was Mr. Hardy's sister, and spent most of her time at his house. When she heard about Clyde Bowden's offer, Aunt Gertrude exclaimed tartly:

"A thousand dollars for finding an old piece of junk! There's something underhanded about such a deal. Mark my words!"

Mrs. Hardy's face wore a worried frown. "I wish your father were here to take the case," she said, "instead of being in Florida."

"Florida!" Joe exclaimed. "Frank, Dad could check on Bowden's credentials. Let's phone him!"

Mrs. Hardy said the detective could be reached only by telegram at an address in Miami. Frank wrote it down and hurriedly sent a wire.

"We may not get an answer for several days," Joe remarked. "I hate to wait. Why can't we make a start on Bowden's case? We can drop it any time we like."

"Okay, but let's not get in too deep until we hear from Dad."

"I'll let Bowden know," said Joe. He dialed the Garden Gate Motel. Bowden was not in, so Joe left a message for him. Then he turned to Frank. "What say we advertise in the newspaper for information about the demiculverin?"

"Good idea." Another call placed a query in the classified section of the Bayport *Times,* which had a wide circulation in the smaller outlying towns.

"Now we're getting some place!" Joe exulted. "Say, maybe Aunt Gertrude can help us."

"How?"

"As newly elected president of the Bayport Historical Society," Joe said, "she might have some information about ancient cannon in the vicinity."

Their aunt had gone to the kitchen to start preparations for lunch, so the boys went out there and put the question to her. After a moment's thought, Miss Hardy said, "I know of one cannon."

"Where is it?" Joe asked eagerly.

"Let me see— I think it's on the back lawn of a museum in Greenville."

"Do you know what type it is?" Frank asked.

"I think it may be pre–Civil War," Aunt Gertrude replied. "It might be Spanish. I'm not sure."

"We'll take a look," said Joe.

After lunch the boys set off in their convertible for the Greenville Museum. It was a small building on the corner of two roads at the edge of town. The main entrance was on one road, with a tall hedge in front of the building. Extensive grounds stretched to the rear on the side road, along which ran a high, iron picket fence. Frank parked in front alongside the hedge, and the brothers walked through a gate to the spacious lawn at the back.

The cannon, a long-barreled six-pounder, stood in the center of the plot. Joe dashed across the flagstones leading to it and read the plaque fixed to the piece.

"It's a Spanish gun!"

Frank joined him and read the inscription on the bronze plaque. It stated:

"Pasavolante, meaning fast action. Made in Toledo, Spain. Often called *cerbatana,* after Cerebus, the fierce dog of mythology. *Pasavolante* in modern Spanish means peashooter."

"Do you suppose this could be the peashooter

that Bowden is searching for and he just got the name wrong?" Joe asked.

"I doubt it," Frank answered. "Bowden seemed sure it was a demiculverin."

"False clue." Joe sighed.

As the brothers started back across the lawn, they noticed a tall, slender man, with a swarthy complexion, entering from a side gate. Bareheaded and wearing a black cotton motorcycle jacket, he moved hurriedly toward the gun.

Casting backward glances, the boys watched him as they continued to the roadway. Now the man was kneeling at the *pasavolante*. Frank and Joe paused long enough to watch him rise and run to the far side of the cannon to scrutinize it.

"Maybe we're not the only ones trying to locate a demiculverin," Joe remarked. "Let's go back and question that fellow."

Retracing their steps, they had covered only a few feet when the man suddenly ran for the side gate by which he had entered.

"He must be goofy," Joe remarked.

The brothers turned back and hurried to the road. The next moment, they heard a motorcycle roar into action.

The swarthy stranger, goggles over his eyes, sped around the corner. He headed directly toward the boys!

CHAPTER III

A Motorcycle Clue

As the motorcycle roared down on them, Frank and Joe leaped aside and stumbled headlong into the hedge. The driver missed them by inches!

"Sorry!" he shouted and sped off.

The boys picked themselves up. Both were angry.

"Did that lunatic mean he was sorry he didn't hit us?" Joe stormed.

"I'd like to get my hands on him!" Frank said. "Look at my trousers!" The sharp twigs of the hedge had made a long tear in them.

"Did you get his license number?" Joe asked.

"No," Frank answered ruefully. "But the motorcycle looked like a foreign make. I saw the letter K on the rear fender."

"If I ever see that fellow again, he'll have some explaining to do as to why he nearly hit us," said

Joe. "And I'd like to ask him about his interest in the old cannon, too."

"He certainly acted as if he was afraid somebody might notice what he was doing," said Frank.

When the boys reached home they hurried into the kitchen. Aunt Gertrude was just removing a batch of cookies from the oven. She glanced over her spectacles and exclaimed, "No need to charge in here like a herd of buffalo!"

"We smelled the cookies and couldn't wait to have some," Joe said with a grin, as he reached for the tray of hot gingersnaps.

This subtle flattery softened the maiden lady's stern demeanor. "Well, in that case, have one," she said. "But don't eat them too fast or you'll get indigestion."

"Indigestion!" Frank cried out. "What did you do? Bake rocks in 'em?"

Aunt Gertrude gave her nephew a withering look. Although she would be the last person to admit it, she enjoyed the boys' teasing. But to hear her scold and correct them, a listener might think Frank and Joe were the bane of her existence. Aunt Gertrude's peppery manner, however, concealed a great depth of affection for them.

"Frank!" she sputtered. "You've torn your trousers!"

"Had a little accident," he admitted, and told her of the motorcyclist.

"I knew it!" Miss Hardy said firmly. "Hoodlums are after you two again. Stay away from such people!"

Frank suppressed a chuckle while Aunt Gertrude took another tray of cookies from the oven. "You wouldn't want us to let 'em run around loose, would you?" he teased.

"Well, don't say I didn't warn you." His aunt sighed. "Trouble, trouble," she added to herself.

"What trouble?" Frank asked.

"The Bayport Historical Society," Aunt Gertrude replied. "What would you do with a case full of swords?"

Frank nearly choked on a cookie. "Swords!"

"Yes, cutlasses. I'd like to keep them."

"Please, Aunty, start from the beginning," Joe begged, "and tell us about it."

Aunt Gertrude explained that the Bayport Historical Society had recently received a gift from the estate of Senator Entwistle. It included some lovely old costumes dating from 1812 and a case of cutlasses.

"I argued with our members," Aunt Gertrude went on, "but they insist that we present the cutlasses to the museum at the state capitol."

"Too bad," said Frank, then asked, "Is it your job to have them shipped?"

"Yes," she replied. "But the cutlasses are to be moved to the basement temporarily. The museum isn't ready to receive them."

"And you'd like us to help you," the boys said in unison.

"Yes. Tomorrow evening."

"We'll be there."

Frank and Joe went to their room and sat down to discuss the next move in locating the cannon which Bowden wanted.

"We can't do anything today out of town," said Frank, glancing at the table clock between the boys' beds. "It's almost time for dinner."

"There's something we *can* do," Joe spoke up. "Visit the motorcycle shops in Bayport and find out the name of the foreign make with a K."

"Good idea, Joe. We may even learn the identity of that fellow who nearly ran us down."

"What are we waiting for? Let's go!" Joe urged.

The boys had better luck than they had anticipated. The first dealer they called on explained that the letter K indicated the motorcycle was the Kesselring, a German make.

"You don't see many of them around," he said. "But they're becoming more popular."

"Do you sell them?" Frank asked.

"No."

"Who does?"

"Nobody in Bayport. And no one in town owns one, either."

"Do you know where the nearest agency is located?" Frank asked.

"Yes," the dealer replied. "In Delmore."

"That's where the penitentiary is," Joe remarked.

The man nodded. "The dealer there mostly sells bikes, but he took on the Kesselring motorcycle agency because the machines come from his native country."

The Hardys exchanged glances. Had the man they had seen on a Kesselring bought his motorcycle in Delmore? The boys thanked the dealer and rode off in their convertible.

"What say we drive over to Delmore in the morning and talk to that agent?" Joe suggested.

"We'll do it," Frank agreed. "The main road there is still closed. The detour leads past the Entwistle place where the cutlasses came from."

At home the boys were greeted by the aroma of fried chicken that their mother was preparing.

"You're just in time," she said, smiling.

The boys washed, then followed Mrs. Hardy and Aunt Gertrude to the table.

"Any word from Dad?" Frank asked a few minutes later.

"No," Mrs. Hardy replied. "But we should hear something soon."

Joe queried Aunt Gertrude about the Entwistle mansion. She said it was supposed to be deserted. "A shame, too, since it's such a beautiful place. One of our Society members hinted that there might be some valuable pieces, which the executors didn't find, in the house. He said Mr.

Entwistle was a queer old duck. There's even talk that tramps stay there sometimes."

That evening the phone rang twice and each time the boys hoped it would be a message from their father. But they were disappointed. Finally Frank and Joe, restless, decided to ride out to the Entwistle mansion and look around.

"Maybe we can find out if there's anything to the talk about the old place," said Frank, as they drove along the detour road toward the old estate.

"Yes—" Joe began, then broke off as the noisy approach of a motorcycle reached his ears. The next moment he exclaimed, "Hey, Frank! That sounds like the Kesselring cycle!"

His brother listened intently. "You're right. Hope he comes this way."

But the Hardys were disappointed when the sound of the motorcycle grew fainter.

"He must have turned down a side road," Joe said. "Let's try to catch up with him."

Frank was about to agree when both boys saw something that made them gasp.

"That red glow in the sky!" Joe exclaimed. "It's right where the Entwistle mansion is!"

"The place must be on fire!" cried out Frank, stepping harder on the accelerator.

Soon they came within sight of the grounds. On a knoll stood the huge house. One wing was a mass of flames!

"We must get the fire department here before the whole place goes up!" said Frank.

He backed the car around, and in a few minutes the boys reached a farmhouse, where they put in a call to Bayport reporting the fire.

Then they sped back to the scene of the blaze. As the brothers got out of the car, they heard sirens wailing. Minutes later several fire engines screamed to a halt before the burning mansion. Shouts of firemen filled the air while they fought to restrict damage to the wing that was being consumed.

Finally, after a half-hour battle, the flames were quenched and the bulk of the big house stood unscathed. Chief Tally, after investigating the charred ruins, returned to his car. A good friend of the Hardys, he greeted the boys with a weary smile. Frank told him they had heard that articles of value might be hidden in the house.

"Could be," the fire chief said. "We suspect an intruder was ransacking the place and dropped a lighted cigarette."

Joe told him of hearing a motorcyclist racing away near the Entwistle place. "He might be the one who was here," he said.

Chief Tally smiled. "You boys are always on the job but this is the quickest I've ever received a clue. If you find out anything else about this rider, let me know."

Frank then told him about the man on the

Kesselring motorcycle who had nearly run the boys down. "The machine we heard tonight had the same kind of roar," he said.

"Thanks. I'll keep the information in mind." The chief nodded, then turned to speak to two firemen who would remain at the mansion, and the boys returned to their convertible.

"Frank," said Joe as they drove home, "if that rider is a housebreaker, he may be interested in cannon for no good reason."

The boys slept well, but the ringing of the telephone early the next morning awakened them. By the time Frank reached the hallway to answer it, he heard his mother talking on the extension in her bedroom. The door was open and she waved him in.

"Fenton, here's Frank now," she said. "You tell him." She turned to her son, excitement in her eyes. "That man Bowden is a fake!" she announced.

CHAPTER IV

New Tactics

"DAD! Hello!" Frank called into the receiver. "How are you? . . . That's good. What's this about Bowden?"

"The man isn't known here in Tampa, Frank."

"You mean he was lying about his work on the pageant?"

"Definitely. No pirate ship with a demiculverin has been entered in the Gasparilla event."

Frank whistled. "I've been suspicious of Bowden from the start. But you don't think we should stop looking for the cannon, do you?"

"Certainly not. Apparently there's a mystery connected with it that's worth looking into. Furthermore, I'm working on a case—swindlers— that Bowden may be mixed up in. Apparently he's using an assumed name."

"Shall we notify the police or shadow him ourselves?" Frank asked.

Mr. Hardy's advice was to do neither. Instead, he advised that his sons continue to be friendly with Bowden and not let him know they had uncovered his lie.

"It's the best way to get at the truth," he said. "And let me know if I can be of any more help. I'd like to speak to your mother again."

Frank dashed back to the boys' room and told his brother the latest news.

"Hot-diggety-dog!" Joe cried, hopping out of bed. "Frank, this is going to be fun. We pretend to play along with Bowden, but all the time we're trying to find out what he's up to!"

Frank stared out the window. "I'm wondering which problem we should tackle first—Bowden or the motorcyclist."

Joe had a suggestion. "Let's combine the two in one trip. We'll go to the motel first, then on to Delmore."

"Okay."

During breakfast with Mrs. Hardy and Aunt Gertrude, the brothers told about their plan, and as soon as they finished eating, started for the door. Aunt Gertrude stopped them and handed Joe a book.

"You boys might as well employ your time profitably while you're riding along. Joe, read this aloud while Frank drives."

Her nephew glanced at the book. "Why, this is great, Aunt Gertrude! It tells about the various types of artillery. Where did you find this book?"

"In your father's library." She chuckled. "I thought it might give you a clue to that demi-culverin you're trying to find."

The boys hugged her, then kissed their mother. "We'll be home in time to move those cutlasses," they promised.

As the brothers rode off, Joe consulted the index of the book. Then he turned to a section on culverins and read aloud:

"It derives from the Latin word *colubra* [snake]. Culverins were highly esteemed on account of their range and effectiveness of fire. Their thick walls, long bores, and heavy powder charges made them the most deadly of field-pieces."

"Fieldpieces!" Frank interrupted. "Why would Bowden want to mount a fieldpiece on a pirate ship?"

Joe grinned. "Maybe he doesn't know any better. Score one for us!"

Half a mile farther along the highway, Frank pulled up in front of the Garden Gate Motel. The clerk was not at his desk when the boys entered, but a maid told them Bowden was in Cabin 15.

The brothers walked down a long row of rooms.

"There it is!" Joe said, spotting the number. He knocked on the door. There was no answer, so he rapped again. Still Bowden did not answer.

"Say, this looks like a note," Joe said, eying a folded bit of white paper pinned below the doorknob.

"Maybe it's for us," Frank suggested.

He and Joe peered at the printed message and opened their eyes wide in amazement. It read:

Bowden! Clear out before it's too late!

"Wow! This fellow has an enemy!" Frank exclaimed.

"Sounds as if he means business, whoever he is," Joe whispered.

In hushed tones the brothers discussed the threat. Why did Bowden have such a deadly enemy? Was it because of the demiculverin?

"This may drive Bowden away," Joe remarked. "Then we'll lose track of him."

Frank shook his head. "I doubt it. He wants that cannon too badly. Well, let's go to Delmore and stop here on our way back."

The detour they had to make took the boys past the farm of their friend Chet Morton. Chet was eighteen, roly-poly, good-natured, and loved to eat. Solving mysteries with the Hardys always gave him the jitters. Despite this, he was a loyal assistant and on more than one occasion had saved them from dangerous predicaments.

"Let's stop a minute," Joe suggested, seeing Chet's sister Iola near the swimming pool.

Frank grinned knowingly. Joe and Iola dated

frequently. He pulled into the driveway. The boys got out and walked toward the pretty dark-haired girl.

"Hi!" she said.

"Hi, yourself!" Joe said. "Where's Chet?"

Iola pointed into the pool. Their stout friend was under water, wearing flippers and a snorkel. He traveled slowly, the snorkel moving like the periscope of a miniature submarine.

"Ahoy!" Joe yelled, as the brothers ran to the water's edge.

Chet continued moving about like a walrus. But finally he emerged and removed the face mask and flippers.

"Hi, fellows!" he called. "I'm having a hard time learning this business. Can't get down deep enough."

"What's the trouble?" Joe asked. "That extra fat you carry around make you too buoyant?" he teased.

"Now, listen here," said Chet, "just because I know good food when I see it—"

He smacked his lips as if imagining he was about to taste something delicious. Then he changed the subject, telling them he was going to take lessons in skin diving from the same man who had taught the Hardys.

"Swell," said Joe.

"I can't start, though, until I earn enough money to buy all the gear."

"Don't let that worry you," Frank spoke up. "I'll lend you my outfit."

"Thanks. And now bring me up to date on everything that's happened lately."

The Hardys had just finished telling Chet and Iola about Bowden, the mysterious cyclist, and the skin-diving attack, when they saw a car driving in. At the wheel sat Callie Shaw, an attractive girl with blond hair and sparkling brown eyes. She was Iola's chum and Frank's regular date.

Callie alighted, and after greeting everyone, said, "I'm glad you're all here. I wanted to talk over plans for our Fourth-of-July beach party. Tony Prito is coming with us too."

Tony, a schoolmate and fellow athlete at Bayport High, had been through many adventures with the Hardys.

"Let's have a clambake like last year," Frank suggested.

"And lobster," Joe added. "Tell you what, Chet. You can put on my diving gear and get us some lobsters."

"Not me," said Chet. "I wouldn't want to tangle with that human devilfish who shot at you fellows."

Iola looked worried. "Do you think he's still lurking around?" she asked.

The Hardys doubted this. "He knows we're

looking for him, so he'll probably keep out of sight," Joe reasoned.

Suddenly Frank grabbed Joe's arm. "Look over there! Someone's spying on us!"

He had seen an intruder peering from behind a tree near the road. The quick glimpse of a black jacket led Frank to believe that the man might be the wanted motorcyclist!

"Come on, Joe!" he whispered, starting to run.

Instantly the man dodged from behind the tree and started to run. The chase was on!

Having the advantage of a head start, he managed to keep ahead of them. When the man reached a parked motorcycle, he jumped on and sped off.

From the silhouette of the rider and the sound of the motor, there was no doubt in the Hardys' minds as to the spy's identity.

"It's the rider we're looking for!" Joe exclaimed.

Together, the brothers ran back to their car and hurried after the suspect. They had covered nearly two miles before they caught sight of the man. Reaching the crest of the next slope, he looked back. Sensing that his pursuers were getting closer, the rider revved his machine and shot out of sight into the curving downgrade.

"Faster!" Joe urged. "He's getting away from us!"

Frank bore down and their car whined around the curve in hot pursuit of the Kesselring. Once again in the open, where the highway stretched out for miles, the boys could no longer see the motorcycle.

"He turned off!" Joe said in disappointment. "But where?"

Frank's brow furrowed. "He couldn't have reached this point," Frank replied. "He must have swung into that dirt road we just passed. Let's go back!"

Screeching to a stop, he made a U turn and sped to the side road. As the car slowed, Joe cried out, "I see a single skid track going in there! That's the place!"

Frank swung the car across the road and they plunged onto the rough, narrow, dirt lane. Fresh motorcycle tracks were clearly evident. Dust filled the air, choking the boys as they sped along.

"Stop!" Joe cried suddenly. "The track ends here!"

Parking the car and locking it, the brothers ran back to the point where the tracks turned off into the pine woods.

"He couldn't go very far through here on his motorcycle," Frank said, as the brothers pressed on excitedly.

"You're right!" Joe whispered a moment later. "Look!"

CHAPTER V

The Stakeout

AHEAD of the Hardys in the deep woods stood a cabin. The Kesselring motorcycle was parked near the front door. Quietly the brothers moved into position for a better view of the one-room building. This must be the hide-out of the suspect!

"End of our search," Joe whispered exultantly.

The brothers moved forward. Frank signaled Joe to cover the rear of the cabin while he went to the front door. It was open and the place appeared to be deserted. Frank strode inside. The rider was not in sight and there was no place where he might be hiding.

"He gave us the slip," said Frank as Joe joined him.

"But not for long," Joe declared. "He'll return for his cycle."

Frank suggested that the boys pretend to leave,

The boys shifted their positions

then double back and stay in hiding until the
man returned.

"Suppose he finds out our car is still on the
road," Joe said.

"We'll have to take that chance," his brother declared.

The boys walked off in the direction of their convertible, but five hundred feet beyond the cabin they turned and quietly made their way back. Hiding behind clumps of brush, they be-

"Get ready, Joe," Frank whispered

gan their vigil. Fifteen minutes went by. Thirty.

Suddenly the quiet of the morning was broken by the crackling sound of approaching footsteps. The Hardys tensed. The person was approaching from behind them. They shifted their position.

"Get ready, Joe," Frank whispered.

The steps grew louder and the figure of a man appeared through the brush. The boys pounced on him, and all three fell hard to the ground. Frank and Joe sprang up immediately to look at their victim.

"Bowden!" Joe gasped.

"For heaven's sake, what ails you guys?" the man stormed, picking himself up.

"We—we thought you were someone else," Joe replied.

"Who?" Bowden demanded.

"We don't know," Frank answered.

"That's ridiculous," Bowden declared scornfully.

"Maybe," said Frank, wondering if Bowden had a rendezvous with the occupant of the cabin. "Why are you here?" he asked.

"I might ask you the same thing," Bowden retorted.

"That's easily answered," Frank said, pointing to the motorcycle. "We want to talk to the man who owns it."

"Do you know him?" Joe asked Bowden.

"Never saw the thing before," he answered.

"Now tell us what brings you here," Frank went on.

"A tip about the demiculverin." Bowden glanced about apprehensively. "It may be buried near here."

Both boys surmised this was another phony story. Bowden was carrying no digging tools, nor was he dressed in work clothes.

"Oh, I know I don't look like a digger," he said, as if reading their thoughts. "I was just looking for a likely place to excavate."

"Who gave you the tip?" Frank asked.

"I can't tell you that. The information was given to me in confidence."

Frank was tempted to ask Bowden why he wanted a fieldpiece for a ship. But recalling his father's admonition, he merely said:

"Sorry we knocked you down, Mr. Bowden. And let us know if you want us to help you dig here."

Joe followed Frank's cue to be pleasant. "We went to the motel to see you this morning," he said. "Frank and I thought we'd talk to you a little more about the cannon you want us to find."

Frank broke in. "We saw the warning note on your door." He watched Bowden closely.

"Warning note?" the man repeated, showing real surprise. After Frank explained, Bowden suddenly laughed. "I guess those kids at the motel were pulling a joke on me. They were playing cops-and-robbers when I left." He glanced at his wrist watch. "I must get back."

He strode off in the direction of the road. Joe turned to Frank. "Do you believe that cops-and-robbers story?"

"No. There wasn't a child around that motel. I think one of us ought to follow Bowden and send the police up here."

"Good idea. You go; I'll stay," Joe offered. "Pick you up later."

While Joe concealed himself to stake out the cabin, Frank cautiously followed the suspect. Presently Bowden got into a car parked some distance ahead of the Hardys' and rode off.

"Wonder where he's going," Frank said to himself. "I'll bet we interrupted some kind of meeting."

He climbed into the convertible and started it. Keeping a discreet distance behind Bowden, so he would not become suspicious, he trailed him. Frank was disappointed when the man went directly to his motel and entered his cabin. He did not come out.

"I'll phone Chief Collig," Frank decided, and drove on to the next gas station to make the call.

He quickly dialed headquarters and talked with the officer. The police chief agreed to send two men to the woods at once to relieve Joe.

"Good work," he said.

Frank returned to the woods and proceeded cautiously to the cabin in case the suspect was hiding nearby. Joe was not in sight. But after Frank gave several birdcalls which they used as signals, Joe emerged from behind a tree.

"Anything doing?" Frank asked.

Joe shook his head, then Frank told him about Bowden and Chief Collig. Ten minutes later the boys were relieved by two plain-clothes men who took over the watch.

The Hardys hurried through the woods and drove on toward Delmore. It was nearly noon when they arrived in that town. Passing the massive stone walls of the state prison, they turned into the business section of town and located the motorcycle shop.

"Good morning," said the short, smiling proprietor who introduced himself as Mr. Braun. "You wish to rent or buy a bike?"

"We're interested in your Kesselrings," Frank replied. "Do you sell them?"

"Yes, I have the agency. But I haven't sold one of those motorcycles in a long time. One's been standing in my basement for weeks. Would you like to see it?"

Frank and Joe looked at each other. Was their clue going to lead nowhere?

Joe said, "Yes, I'd like to see it."

Mr. Braun opened a trap door in the floor, clicked on a light switch, and the three descended a flight of wooden stairs. The man walked around a high pile of cartons, then suddenly exclaimed:

"*Ach, Himmel!*"

"What's the matter?" Frank asked.

The proprietor clapped a hand to his head. "My Kesselring! It's gone! Stolen!"

Mr. Braun excitedly went on to say that he had been on a vacation for two weeks and had just returned. The Kesselring had been there when he left.

"*Ach,* what will I do?" he wailed. "I never should have closed my shop!"

Frank laid a hand on the man's shoulder. "You may get the motorcycle back this very day," he said. He told of finding the one at the cabin, and that policemen were now at the spot waiting to capture the thief. The dealer was overjoyed at the news.

Frank at once telephoned this latest development to Chief Collig, while Mr. Braun thanked the boys repeatedly. Then they said good-by and left. After a quick lunch at a nearby diner, the Hardys returned to their convertible.

"Joe, I have a hunch," said Frank. "That motorcycle thief might be a recently released inmate of the penitentiary. Mr. Braun's shop here in Delmore would be a likely place for him to rob. Let's call on Warden Duckworth and ask him some questions."

"Good idea."

The warden was an old friend of Mr. Hardy, and the boys had once assisted him in solving a prison break. Reaching the penitentiary, Frank called him from the main gate phone. A guard accompanied them to Warden Duckworth's office, where the official greeted them cordially.

"What brings you way out here from Bayport?" he asked.

Frank told him their suspicions and said, "We'd like to find out the names of men released from here within the past two weeks."

Warden Duckworth rose, walked to his filing cabinet, checked the records, and returned with some forms. "We've let six men go," he replied. "Four old-timers and a couple of young fellows. All had served their time."

"We can forget about the old-timers," Frank said. "The man we suspect is probably in his twenties. Who were the young ones?"

"One is Bob Chidsie, a car thief. The other, Hal Latsky, a safecracker."

"May we see their pictures?" Frank asked.

"Certainly." Duckworth handed over the record cards, to which small photos were attached.

"That's the motorcycle thief!" Joe said immediately, pointing to Latsky.

Frank looked thoughtful. "Don't forget, Joe, we've never seen this fellow close up without his goggles. Warden, could you tell us something more about him?"

"Yes—" The man studied Latsky's card for a moment. "Besides safecracking, he's an explosives expert. Also, he has an unusual hobby—the study of ancient cannon!"

CHAPTER VI

Profitable Sleuthing

AT THE mention of Latsky's interest in ancient cannon, Frank cried out, "That convinces me, Warden! Latsky is the man we're after."

Once more the Hardys telephoned Chief Collig, who was even more amazed than before at the brothers' sleuthing. "We'll have you on the force yet!" he said jokingly.

He gave them a report on the stakeout in the woods. Having learned from Braun the manufacturer's serial numbers of the stolen motorcycle, the chief had short-waved them to his men at the cabin. They, in turn, had made positive identification of the motorcycle.

"It's the stolen Kesselring all right," said the police chief. "The thief hasn't returned yet, but we'll maintain a round-the-clock surveillance for as long as we need it. Braun has agreed to cooperate by leaving the motorcycle there awhile as bait for the thief. He might try to get it back."

Before the Hardys left, Warden Duckworth gave them pictures of Latsky. "Give these to Chief Collig," he requested.

On the way to Bayport the boys discussed the strange turn of events. If Latsky were the motorcycle rider, was he trailing the Hardys because they were searching for an old cannon? Did he know Bowden, and had the two planned a meeting in the woods? Or were they enemies, both looking for the old demiculverin?

"I'm going to phone Warden Duckworth and see if he can tell us anything about Bowden," said Frank.

When the boys reached home, Frank immediately put in the call. The warden said he had no released prisoner on his list named Bowden, nor had he ever heard Latsky mention anyone by that name.

"I'll ask the guards and prisoners, though," Warden Duckworth promised. An hour later he called back. "If Latsky knows anyone named Bowden, he never mentioned it here."

"Thanks, anyway," said Frank and hung up.

He was disappointed not to have uncovered another clue but turned his attention to Aunt Gertrude who had just come in the front door. She was waving three letters.

"I picked these up from the box at the newspaper office," she said, handing them over. "You forgot all about your ad. I suppose these are some answers from cranks. Well, hurry up and open them. I'm entitled to know what's inside!"

Frank smiled as he tore open the first envelope. Joe came to stand beside him, and read over his brother's shoulder.

The writer of the first note proved to be the amusing old artillery sergeant who had set off the mortar in the town square the day before. Sergeant Tilton said that he lived up the coast near Pirates' Hill. He had once heard there was an old cannon on the hill, but it had been buried by sand in a storm many years ago—long before Tilton's birth.

"That's a swell lead!" Joe exclaimed enthusiastically.

"I don't know," said Frank. "Sergeant Tilton thinks up such tall tales you can't be sure when he's telling another whopper."

Both boys agreed that the message should be investigated, nevertheless.

The second letter came from Mr. Maglan, the retired custodian of the Bayport Historical Society. Frank opened it.

"Wait till you hear this, Aunty." He chuckled.

"Why, what is it?"

"Mr. Maglan says three old cannons have been stored in the cellar of the Historical Society's building for thirty years! The new custodian, Mr. Lightbody, evidently doesn't know about them."

"What!" exclaimed Miss Hardy. "Cannons in the basement!"

Joe roared with laughter. "Why, Aunt Gertrude, you've been sitting right above three loaded guns all these years without knowing it. I always thought you knew everything about the Bayport Historical Society building."

The boys' aunt did not laugh. "This is serious. Suppose there is powder in them!" she cried out. "Why—"

Frank assured her that thirty-year-old gunpowder would be damp and harmless. Aunt Gertrude merely said "Humph!" and then reminded her nephews tartly about carrying the cutlasses to the basement. "Mr. Lightbody says they're in the way."

"We'll go right after supper," Joe said. "And we'll investigate those old cannons at the same time."

The third note was of more serious import. Letters of the alphabet had been cut from newspapers and pasted on the paper to form words.

The message, sent anonymously, bore no signature—nor a mark to indicate one. It read:

> *Look for the cannon at your own risk. If you're smart you'll drop Bowden's case.*

"Wow! Things are really getting complicated!" Joe exclaimed. "The camps are lining up."

"Yes," Frank agreed. "And the writer must have found out we're the ones who put that ad in the paper."

"I don't like this!" Aunt Gertrude declared. "The case is becoming too dangerous. If you boys don't give it up, you may have someone shooting a cannon at you!"

When Mrs. Hardy heard about the threat, she too became alarmed. Both she and Aunt Gertrude appealed to the boys to drop the case, at least until their father returned from Florida.

"We can't stop work now," Frank protested. "Joe and I are just getting some good leads. And anyway, Dad wants us to work on the case. But we promise you we'll be careful."

Both women sighed. Then Aunt Gertrude said, "Well, Laura, I suppose with three men against us—and one of them my brother—we'll have to give in. But I want to go on record as saying that if you boys get hurt, you can't blame—"

The ringing of the telephone interrupted Aunt Gertrude's tirade. Joe grabbed up the phone and everyone waited tensely.

"Maybe it's Fenton," Mrs. Hardy whispered.

Frank noticed Joe's jaws tighten as he listened to the message. It could not be a call from their father.

"Frank," Joe whispered, "come here! It's Bowden. He wants to talk to you, too."

His brother put his ear close to the phone. "Hello," he said, "this is Frank."

Bowden's voice sounded scared. "Listen! You've got to help me! I've been threatened!"

"By whom?" Frank asked. "Those kids again?"

"No, no. This is for real!" Bowden's voice was shaky and faint. But suddenly it became strong again. "Fr-ank! Joe!" he cried out.

"Were you threatened by someone named Latsky?" Frank demanded.

There was no answer.

"Mr. Bowden?" Frank said questioningly.

Still there was no response, but suddenly the Hardys heard a thud and the noise of a phone dropping onto a hard surface.

"Hello! Hello!" Frank kept saying.

There was dead silence for another moment. Then a strange voice said ominously into the instrument:

"You Hardy boys! Drop the cannon search at once! This is your last warning!"

The threat ended with a sharp click in the Hardys' receiver as the intruder in Bowden's cabin slammed down the telephone.

Frank whirled to face his brother. "It sounds as if Bowden had been attacked! Probably by the person who just gave us that final warning!"

Joe started for the door. "Let's hurry over to Bowden's motel. We may catch the guy."

Frank thought it best to get help to Bowden

immediately. "He may be seriously injured. I'll notify the desk clerk at the Garden Gate."

With frantic haste, Frank dialed the motel office number, but the line was busy.

"Come on!" Joe urged impatiently. "We can get there in a few minutes if we hurry."

The brothers ran to the convertible. When they reached the motel, Frank pulled up in front of Cabin 15. The door stood ajar and the brothers burst inside.

Bowden lay face down on the floor, unconscious. Blood trickled from the back of his head!

CHAPTER VII

Mysterious Attackers

As Joe and Frank rushed over to Bowden, the man groaned slightly and moved his arms. Frank turned him over.

"I'll get some water," Joe offered, and hurried to the bathroom for it.

He filled a glass and sprinkled some of the water against the prostrate man's neck and face. Bowden shook his head dazedly as he regained consciousness, and the boys helped him to his feet.

"How did you—?" he stammered, recognizing them. "Where's—? Oh, my head!"

Frank assisted Bowden to the bed, where Joe applied an antiseptic bandage he had found in the bathroom medicine chest. Then they began to question him. Bowden said he had not seen his attacker.

"I hadn't locked my door," he explained.

"Somebody must have sneaked up from behind and hit me with a blackjack!"

"Latsky?" Frank queried, watching Bowden narrowly.

"Never heard of him," he replied.

"Who threatened you?" Joe asked.

"I don't know. An unsigned note had been shoved under my door. It's right—" Bowden looked toward the telephone stand. "Why—" he sputtered. "It's gone! It was right there!"

"Your attacker must have taken it," said Joe.

Frank telephoned the desk clerk to report the assault. The clerk said he had not seen anybody prowling around, and promised to notify the local police at once.

As Bowden's condition improved, the brothers tried to ferret out more information from their mysterious client. "Where did you say you live in Tampa?" Joe inquired.

"I didn't say. Why do you ask?"

Joe explained that he thought Bowden's family or friends should be notified in case of serious trouble.

"Forget it," Bowden replied with a wave of the hand. "I haven't any family."

The man's reluctance to tell where he lived seemed to confirm Mr. Hardy's suspicion that Bowden might be mixed up with a group of swindlers. But the brothers gave no sign of this.

"About the demiculverin," Frank went on. "I

read that it's a fieldpiece and not used on ships."

Bowden was startled for a moment but regained his composure by pulling out a cigar. Lighting it, he said, "I admire your thoroughness. But I didn't want the cannon for a ship, only for a pageant—as part of the shore batteries."

"Oh," Frank said nonchalantly, "then the demiculverin isn't too important."

"What?"

"If it's just for a dummy shore battery, you can rig up a wooden one," Frank added.

"But—but, boys!" Bowden's face grew red with excitement. "I must have the old cannon. Everything has to be authentic."

He laid a firm hand on Frank's arm. "You must help me! I'll double the reward. How about two thousand dollars?"

"It's not the money, Mr. Bowden," Frank replied. "It's just that—"

"All right, I'll co-operate better," he said pleadingly.

"For example?"

"I can't reveal all my secrets, but I feel certain the cannon will be found along the shore here," Bowden declared.

"We'll do our best," Frank promised.

When the police arrived, the boys told them all they knew about the attack on Bowden but said nothing about the threat to themselves. Then they left.

"What do you make of it?" Joe asked his brother as they drove away from the motel.

"This mystery is getting more complicated by the minute," Frank replied. "Bowden has an enemy all right, and he's lying when he says he doesn't know who he is."

On the way home the boys noticed another convertible following them. In the rear-view mirror, Frank saw that the slender, good-looking young man driver was alone.

"Do you think he's trailing us?" Frank asked, as the car remained fifty feet behind the Hardys' for about half a mile.

"Why don't you find out? Slow down and see if he'll pass," Joe suggested.

Frank did so. The other driver pulled out and zoomed ahead. As he passed the Hardy car, he stared hard at the boys.

"Did you recognize him, Frank?"

"Never saw him before."

When the brothers arrived home, Aunt Gertrude told them that the Historical Society had just decided to hold a special meeting that evening. "You can drive me to the meeting and carry the cutlasses to the basement while you're there," she said.

After supper Frank and Joe accompanied Miss Hardy to the meeting place. When they pulled into the parking lot in the rear of the old stone building, several members were going in the front entrance.

As Miss Hardy alighted, she pointed to a basement window which was open. "Such carelessness!" she sputtered. "I must speak to Mr. Lightbody! Frank—Joe, please close it when you're in the basement. Humph! The whole place'll be full of stray cats!"

Her nephews grinned, followed their aunt to the front of the building, and went inside.

"The cutlasses are at the rear of that corridor," Aunt Gertrude said, pointing. "Carry them down to the basement and don't disturb our meeting!" Then she walked briskly into the auditorium.

Frank and Joe went down the corridor. At the end of it stood the case of six cutlasses from the Entwistle estate. The brothers lifted out two of the short swords and examined them.

"Boy, the real thing!" Joe remarked in a low voice. "They're heavy. And look at this edge, Frank." Taking an old envelope from his pocket he sliced it in half with an effortless motion.

"I'd say these are more dangerous than the cannon," Frank murmured. "Maybe that's why some of the Society members want to get rid of them."

"How about a look at the heavy artillery?" Joe said as the boys replaced the cutlasses in the case.

They looked about for the custodian to show them the basement entrance, but could not locate him. "I guess we can find our way," Frank said.

He walked over to a door and pulled it gingerly. Instead of leading to the basement, it opened into the auditorium.

Aunt Gertrude was on the dais, gavel in hand. "The meeting will come to order," she said with authority, and the ensuing bang made it plain that she meant every word.

As the members quickly quieted, Frank saw the custodian seated in the front row. He was a small, thin man with gray hair and a wispy mustache. The boys decided not to bother him.

"Let's try this door," Joe said, walking across the corridor. He turned the knob. The door yawned open into pitch blackness.

"This is the basement entrance, all right." He reached inside for the light switch and flicked it on. There was no response.

"I guess the bulb's burned out," Joe said. "I'll get a flashlight from the car, Frank."

He hurried outside and brought back a powerful flashlight which the boys carried in their car at all times. As Joe beamed it down the steps, Frank lifted the case of cutlasses to his shoulder.

"Lead the way, Joe."

Joe preceded his brother slowly down the cellar steps. "Careful, Frank," he warned. "They're steep."

The next moment Joe pitched forward. A blow

on the side of his head had knocked him unconscious.

"Joe, what happened?" Frank cried as the
flashlight flew forward and rolled under a table.

In the feeble light Frank missed his footing
and lost his balance. The case of cutlasses fell
from his shoulder and landed with a jangling
crash. Frank banged his head full force on the
case and blacked out.

His outcry and the crash of the case threw the
Historical Society meeting into an uproar. Mr.
Lightbody jumped to his feet.

At the same time Aunt Gertrude pounded her
gavel for order. "Keep calm. I'll find out what's
wrong downstairs. Come, Mr. Lightbody! Vice
President, please take the chair!"

Miss Hardy charged to the basement door
ahead of the custodian and felt her way down the
steps. "Frank! Joe!" she called.

Groping in the darkness, she found the flashlight which was still beaming. Waving it around,
she gasped.

*Dashing for the open window was a man in a
motorcycle jacket, a mask over his face.*

In his arms were five cutlasses, which had been
hurled from the case. The sixth lay on the floor.
Beyond it were the two brothers, motionless.

Quickly sizing up the situation, Aunt Gertrude
reached down for the free cutlass, at the same

time crying, "You scoundrel! What have you done to my nephews?"

With a flailing motion, she slapped the man's back with the broad side of the cutlass. He shoved her back.

"Oh, no, you don't!" she cried out.

Thwack! She hit him again. Terrified, the man dropped the five cutlasses with a din heard in the meeting room upstairs and leaped to the sill. As he started to crawl through the window, Aunt Gertrude whacked him again!

CHAPTER VIII

The Battle of Bayport

WITH the intruder gone, Miss Hardy turned her attention to Frank and Joe.

"Where's the electrical panel, Mr. Lightbody?" she asked.

"Under the stairs." He found it and reported that the basement switch had been pulled, probably by the intruder. The custodian flicked the handle up and the place was flooded with light.

"What happened?" someone called out from the top of the stairs. "Do you need help?"

"Call the police," said Miss Hardy, as she began to chafe her nephews' wrists and the backs of their necks. They soon regained consciousness.

The only injuries the boys had sustained were bruises on their heads. Joe surmised that he had been hit with a blackjack.

After Aunt Gertrude had given a brief description of the assailant, Frank said tersely, "Sounds like Latsky. Let's check for clues to make sure."

As they searched, Mr. Lightbody said the basement windows were always locked. The intruder must have forced one open.

Chief Collig arrived in a few minutes and heard the complete story from Aunt Gertrude. "Frank and Joe think it was Latsky," she concluded.

The officer agreed. But a search outside the building failed to reveal any clues except footprints.

"Let's look for fingerprints, boys," Chief Collig suggested. He got his kit from the prowl car and the three searched the basement with no results.

"Latsky must have worn gloves," the officer finally decided.

"I didn't notice," Aunt Gertrude and Mr. Lightbody said together.

An instant later Frank leaned down and cried out, "Here's a button from the fellow's jacket!" On the floor near the open basement window lay a triangular black button imprinted with a motorcycle wheel. "It *was* Latsky!"

Chief Collig dropped the button in his pocket. As he started to leave, the officer said, "The motorcycle rider hasn't returned yet to the cabin. But I'm hoping he may show up there soon."

After Collig had gone, Joe turned to his aunt. "We haven't thanked you for saving us and the cutlasses." He chuckled. "You won the Battle of Bayport, Aunt Gertrude!"

"Oh, tush!" she said, starting upstairs. "Mr. Lightbody, lock and bar that window. Frank and Joe, put those cutlasses back in the case."

When Mr. Lightbody and the boys climbed the stairs a few minutes later, they found Aunt Gertrude surrounded by members of the Historical Society, praising her for her winning the "Battle of Bayport."

"It was nothing," she insisted. "Now we'll resume the meeting."

All the members followed her inside the auditorium except Mr. Lightbody. "Boys, I can tell you about a real Battle of Bayport."

He explained that in reading pirate lore, he had learned that in 1756 a buccaneer ship had attacked two armed merchantmen off Bayport. One of the trading vessels had been sunk with all the officers and crew lost. The other merchantman had managed to sail away.

"The pirate ship," Mr. Lightbody continued, "had had so much of her sail raked by the cannon of the merchantmen that she was unable to give chase. Instead, for some unknown reason, she sent a landing party ashore. Some time later the party returned aboard and the pirate ship limped off."

"Where did this happen?" Joe asked.

"Off Pirates' Hill," Mr. Lightbody replied. "The hill is really named after that incident."

Frank and Joe eyed each other with a smile. Maybe there *was* a basis for Jim Tilton's account of the cannon buried in the sand!

"That's quite a story," said Frank. "And now we'd like to see the old cannons in the basement."

Mr. Lightbody led the way down another stairway and unlocked a door to a dusty, vaultlike room. Three old weapons, green with age, were set up in a row on oak mounts.

"All three are British pieces," the custodian said. "They're a *minion,* a *saker,* and a *pedrero.* And they are all made of cast bronze."

"What queer names!" Joe exclaimed. "Do they mean anything special?"

"The *saker* was named after the saker hawk, one of the fiercer birds used in falconry. The *pedrero*—you notice that it's longer than the others—is relatively lighter because it was used to hurl stone projectiles. Its walls are thinner than those of other guns. The *minion* is the smallest."

"They have beautiful decorations," Joe observed.

The pieces were covered with flower-and-leaf designs. Atop the *saker,* at its balance point, was a handle in the shape of a dolphin.

"This handle," Mr. Lightbody explained, "was used for lashing or lifting the piece. And cannon like these often had colorful nicknames set in raised letters on the barrel. For instance, *The Terror, The Angry One,* or *The Avenger.*"

"This first one is marked *The Wasp*," Joe re-marked. The other cannons bore no names. "Thanks, Mr. Lightbody."

He locked the door and led the way upstairs. Reaching the hall, Frank whispered to Joe, "That clue to the demiculverin petered out. Let's try Pirates' Hill next."

"Right. We'll go there tomorrow."

Just then Aunt Gertrude, followed by the other Society members, came from the meeting room. The boys' aunt was beaming.

"The Society has just voted to present us with one of the cutlasses," she told them.

Frank and Joe grinned in delight. "Great!" said Frank, and Joe added, "It'll be a swell souvenir of the Battle of Bayport! Let's take the one you used to scare off the thief!"

He ran downstairs to get it.

The Hardys returned home directly and Joe made a rack for the prized cutlass. Frank hung the weapon on the stairway wall.

"Looks good," Joe remarked. "I think Dad will like it."

As the brothers prepared for bed, they discussed the masked thief's reason for wanting the cutlasses. Frank and Joe could come to no conclusion and finally they fell asleep.

Next morning after breakfast the boys made plans for their trip to Pirates' Hill.

"Bowden seemed pretty sure the demiculverin's somewhere around there," Frank mused. "I'm going to try getting some more information from him before we leave."

He went to the phone and called the Garden Gate Motel. As Joe stood by, he saw an expression of disbelief cross his brother's face. A moment later Frank hung up.

"Bad news," he said. "Bowden checked out early this morning!"

Joe stared at his brother as if dazed. Then he asked, "Florida?"

"He left no forwarding address."

As soon as the boys collected their wits, they decided to postpone their trip to Pirates' Hill to try to find Bowden. They would go the rounds of local gas stations, hoping to find that Bowden had stopped at one of them and might have left a clue to his destination.

They visited one after another without result. As the brothers were about to return home in dismay, Joe said:

"Frank, there's a gas station about two miles out of town on Route 7. Bowden may have stopped there."

The boys headed for the place and a few minutes later pulled in. A boy was in attendance and they told him to fill their tank.

"Say," said Frank to him, "did a man stop here this morning in a green coupé?"

"Yep," the attendant replied.

"Was he about thirty-five years old, stocky build, and did he have wiry black hair?"

"Yep."

Frank said they were trying to find him and wondered where he had gone. "Did he happen to tell you?"

"Yep. Said he had a big business deal over in Taylorville."

Elated, the Hardys grinned broadly and thanked the boy. Frank paid him and they hurried off.

"Our luck has changed!" Joe remarked.

"I hope we can make Taylorville before Bowden pulls out of there too," Frank said.

Without breaking the speed limit, Frank kept the convertible at a steady pace and they reached Taylorville at twelve o'clock. The town was a fair-sized one, and the streets swarmed with cars and people during the lunch-hour rush.

The Hardys began a systematic search for Bowden's car, going up one street and down another. After they had exhausted the business area, they started on the residential section.

"I see it!" Joe cried out presently.

Bowden's green coupé was parked in front of an old-fashioned house which advertised that luncheons and dinners were served there.

"Maybe he's eating," Joe remarked. "What say we park our car around the corner so he won't spot it?"

Frank agreed this was a good idea and kept going. He pulled into a secluded, dead-end street and locked the convertible. As they walked back toward the restaurant, Frank suddenly grabbed his brother's arm. "We'd better duck. Here he comes!"

"Where?" Joe asked.

"From that house down the street—the big white one."

The brothers stepped back of a hedge and watched the suspect. He went directly toward his car but did not get in. Instead, Bowden turned into the walk which led to the restaurant and disappeared inside.

"What a break!" said Frank. "Joe, you watch the restaurant. I'll go over to that big white house and see what I can find out about Bowden's activities."

Fortunately, the restaurant was almost completely screened from the street by tall trees and shrubbery. There was little chance of Bowden seeing the Hardys.

"What'll I do if Bowden suddenly comes out?" Joe asked.

"Run for our car and give two blasts on the horn. I'll come out and join you, so we can follow him."

Frank hurried across the street, planning his campaign at the neighboring house. "I'll pretend to be a salesman," he told himself.

A thin, white-haired man answered his ring. Smiling, Frank asked if he were Mr. Chestnut. When the man shook his head, Frank asked if he knew where Mr. Chestnut lived.

"Never heard of anybody by that name around here," the elderly man said. He chuckled. "But you came close, son. My name's Ash."

Frank laughed, then said he was a salesman and wondered how he was going to find Mr. Chestnut.

"Sorry I can't help you, young fellow." Mr. Ash smiled. "And I can't buy anything from you. I just spent all my money. A salesman was here a few minutes ago and sold me some stock."

Frank's heart leaped. He was learning more than he had bargained for!

CHAPTER IX

Pirates' Hill

WITHOUT seeming to be too inquisitive, Frank asked Mr. Ash, "Was it oil stock you bought?"

The elderly man shook his head. "It was mining stock. The Copper Slope Mining Company. Ever hear of it?"

Frank said that he had. As a matter of fact, his father owned some of the stock. So Mr. Bowden was not selling phony stock!

"I'll bet Dad will be surprised at this," he thought, then said aloud, "Where could I find the salesman if I should want to buy some stock?"

Mr. Ash told him the man's name was Bowden and he was staying at the Garden Gate Motel in Bayport. "That's where he told me to phone him if I wanted any more stock."

Frank was so amazed that he almost blurted out the fact that Bowden was no longer at the Garden Gate Motel. He thanked Mr. Ash for his courtesy, then walked quickly down the street. Joining his brother, he told him what he had learned. Joe was equally amazed and puzzled. Though the stock was high grade, still the transaction seemed strange.

"We'll wait for Bowden and trail him," Frank stated.

It was not long before the suspect came out of the restaurant and got into his car. Frank and Joe dashed around the corner and hopped into their convertible. The trail led toward Bayport, and when they reached the town, Bowden not only turned into the Garden Gate Motel, but went to Cabin 15, unlocked it, and stepped inside.

"Well, can you beat that!" Joe said.

The boys parked and went in to speak to the clerk who had given Frank the information about Bowden's leaving. The man looked at Frank in surprise.

"I thought you said Mr. Borden on the phone," he explained. "Sorry. Mr. Bowden is still in Cabin 15."

The boys went to see him and held a casual conversation about Pirates' Hill, saying they were going to start searching that area the next day. Did Bowden have any suggestions for them?

"No, I haven't," he replied. "But I'm glad to hear you're going to start work. I don't know how long I can wait around here."

"Are you thinking of leaving soon?" Joe asked

as casually as he could, hoping for information.

"Oh, not right away," Bowden answered. "But it's taking a lot of my valuable time to stay here trying to find that demiculverin."

"I understand," said Frank. "Well, we'll let you know what we find out."

Since it was too late to search on Pirates' Hill that day, the boys went home. They gathered various kinds of tools together which they would use for their digging and put them in the convertible.

"We'll have to take time out from the picnic to make a search," said Frank.

Shortly after breakfast the next morning, the Hardy phone rang. Frank answered the call. It was from Mr. Lightbody. In a highly excited voice the curator cried out:

"The Historical Society's building was broken into late last night. The cutlasses have been stolen!"

"Stolen!" Frank cried out unbelievingly. "How did the thief get in?"

Mr. Lightbody said a rear door of the building had been forced.

"Joe and I will be right over," said Frank and hung up.

The whole Hardy family was upset by the news. Aunt Gertrude declared she was going along.

"I feel a personal responsibility for those cut-lasses," she said.

She and the boys set off at once. By the time they reached the Historical Society building, Chief Collig was there.

"This certainly is unfortunate," he said. "I can't understand how that thief got in here so easily."

"Don't forget Latsky is a safecracker," Joe reminded the chief.

"Wait a second," Frank said. "Let's not jump to conclusions. We don't know for certain that it was Latsky who broke in here the second time."

Chief Collig agreed with the boy's reasoning. He said he would put extra men on the case and notify the state police to be on the lookout for Latsky.

"Neither he nor anyone else has shown up at the cabin in the woods," the officer reported. "I had a hunch the man would come back, but apparently I was wrong."

Hearing this, Frank asked worriedly, "But you're not going to take the stakeout away, are you?"

"No, but I believe the fellow knows we're watching the place and won't return."

At that moment there was a loud booming of the old mortar in the town square. Frank and Joe looked at each other and smiled. They had com-

pletely forgotten that it was Independence Day!
They had planned to watch the parade, then start
off for the picnic.

It was eleven o'clock when they reached home
to pack their car. Mrs. Hardy had left two large
cakes for them—a chocolate and an angel food.
Joe put them into the convertible while Frank
consulted a book on tides in the Bayport area.
Coming out to Joe, he said:

"I guess we can't take the *Sleuth* after all. The
water will be too shallow near Pirates' Hill. It
will be low tide in the middle of the day."

"How about asking Tony to take us in his
Napoli?" Joe suggested. "It draws much less water
than the *Sleuth*."

"Good idea, Joe. I'll call him." He went to the
phone.

"Sure, we can take the *Napoli*," Tony said. "I'll
meet you at the dock."

The Hardys drove off, heading first for the
Morton farm. Chet and Iola were waiting for
them, with several baskets of food which included
lobsters and a sack of clams. Their next stop was
for Callie Shaw, then they drove directly to the
waterfront.

"Hi!" cried Tony, giving his friends an expan-
sive grin. The *Napoli* was chugging quietly at her
berth.

After the food and digging tools had been transferred to the craft and the Hardys had brought

their diving gear from the *Sleuth,* everyone stepped aboard and Tony shoved off.

"I'm sure glad you asked me to go along," he said. "It was going to be a dull day for me without a date."

As the motorboat skimmed along the bay toward the ocean, Callie suddenly began to laugh. The others looked up and followed her eyes to the stern. There stood Chet, a black patch over one eye and a bandanna around his head.

"Yo-ho-ho!" he sang out. "I'm the pirate of Bayport Bay and I'll show you in a few minutes where a vast treasure is hidden!"

The others roared with laughter and Iola added, "A skin diving pirate! You'd better bring up a real treasure or you'll forfeit all second helpings as punishment!"

When they reached the end of the bay and turned up the coast, the young people watched for Pirates' Hill. Minutes later they saw it in the distance. The hill was a desolate hump of sand-covered stone jutting into the sea. There was not a house in sight, except one small cottage about half a mile beyond the crown of the hill.

"That must be Sergeant Tilton's place," Frank remarked.

Tony stopped the *Napoli* some distance off shore and said he was going to test the depth with a pole before going any closer toward land.

"Say, how about my trying out the diving

equipment now?" Chet asked. He removed the bandanna and eye patch. "I want to find that treasure for you."

Grinning, Frank helped Chet adjust the equipment. As the stout boy got into the tank harness, Frank found that he had to punch a hole at the very end of the weighted cartridge belt in order to accommodate Chet's paunchy midriff.

"I think I'll put my gear on, too, in case Chet runs into trouble," said Joe.

He quickly strapped his air tanks into position and the two boys stepped to the gunwale.

"Hold it!" said Tony. "A guy in a motorboat over there is waving at us frantically. Wonder what's up."

"Who is he?" Frank asked.

"I've never seen the fellow before," Tony replied as the boat hove alongside.

Frank called out to the newcomer, a fisherman about fifty, and asked him what was wrong.

"I'm glad I got to you folks in time," the stranger replied. He spoke excitedly. "I just spotted a giant sting ray near here while I was fishing."

"A sting ray!" Frank echoed in surprise. "Well, thanks for telling us. We'll stay out of the water."

Tony pulled a pole from the bottom of the motorboat and asked Frank to test the depth from the prow of the *Napoli*. Then slowly he steered the boat shoreward.

All this time Joe had been casting his eyes over the large expanse of water. There was no sign of the sting ray. Finally he said aloud:

"Do you suppose that man was trying to scare us away from here?"

"What do you mean?" asked Callie.

"Well, a lot of funny things have been going on lately," said Joe. "It wouldn't surprise me if that fellow had some reason for not wanting us to go into the water."

He found binoculars in a compartment and trained them on the other boat which by now was a good distance away. The craft lacked both a name and Coast Guard identification number.

"That fisherman isn't alone!" Joe exclaimed. "I just saw another man's head pop out from under the tarpaulin!"

"Can you see his face?" Frank asked.

"No. He's getting up now, but his back's turned to us."

The Hardys and their friends looked at one another questioningly. Someone had deliberately been hiding from the group. Why? And who was he?

CHAPTER X

A Spy

"LET'S FIND out who those two men are!" Joe urged.

"You mean go after them?" Tony asked.

When Joe nodded, Tony started the motor and the *Napoli* skimmed across the water. Joe kept the binoculars trained on the mysterious fishermen. Suddenly they seemed to realize that the young people were heading directly toward them. Like a flash the man who had remained hidden before dived under the tarpaulin in the bottom of the boat.

The other man started the engine. Then, in a roar which carried across the waves, the boat raced off.

"Wow!" Chet exclaimed. "Some speedy craft!"

"I'll say it is!" said Frank. "That's no ordinary fishing boat!"

The *Napoli* was fast but not fast enough to

overtake the other boat. After a chase of a mile, the other craft was out of sight.

"Guess it's hopeless," said Tony in disgust. He turned back to Pirates' Hill.

The young people continued to discuss the men's strange actions until they were back at the beach. Then Chet said, "Let's forget the mystery. If I don't eat pretty soon—"

Joe grinned and finished the sentence for him. "You'll faint, fall in the water, and a man eating shark will make away with you."

Everyone laughed but Chet. He frowned and added pleadingly, "What's a picnic for, anyway, if you don't eat?"

"We'll take care of that," his sister promised.

Tony anchored the *Napoli* in a scallop-shaped cove, and the young people waded ashore, carrying the baskets of food with them. The waves lapped the beach gently.

"This is an ideal spot for a beach party," said Callie enthusiastically.

She and Iola took charge and gave orders to the boys. Frank and Tony were asked to collect driftwood, while Chet and Joe gathered plenty of seaweed. In a few minutes they returned, their arms full.

"What'll we do with this?" Joe asked.

"Those rocks over there will make a good place for the fire," said Callie.

She found a natural pit among the rocks. Into

it the boys piled the driftwood and started a fire. Soon there was a roaring blaze. Then Frank heaped more rocks into the fire.

When the stones were glowing red and the flames had died out, the boys placed a layer of seaweed over them. Then the girls laid the lobsters and clams in rows on it and piled several more layers of the stringy green kelp over them.

"I can hardly wait," Chet groaned hungrily, as the tantalizing aroma of the sea food reached his nostrils.

While the food was steaming, the rest of the lunch was brought out. The meal started with tomato juice and small sandwiches of ham and chicken. As they ate, the Hardy boys brought their friends up to date on Bowden, Latsky, and the search for the demiculverin.

"Later today Joe and I want to climb to the top of Pirates' Hill and take a look for the cannon," Frank told them.

"We'd better go now," said Joe, grinning. "After this picnic we won't be able to climb!"

A few minutes later Iola announced that the clams and lobsters were ready. The young people gathered around the pit as Joe cleared away the hot seaweed.

"Right this way, folks!" he called out. "First plateful of juicy sizzling hot clams goes to Miss Iola Morton!"

One by one the picnickers came forward and piled their plates. Every clam and lobster disappeared. Then a huge watermelon was cut into sections and served along with Mrs. Hardy's cakes.

Forty minutes later Chet rolled over on the sand. "I can't move!" he moaned.

"Neither can I!" Joe echoed, sprawling full length on his back. "Girls, that was the greatest meal I ever ate!"

There was little conversation during the next hour. Chet was soon snoring and the others stretched out for a rest. But finally they arose and walked toward the water's edge. Chet was the last to join the group.

"How about my doing that skin diving now?" he suggested.

"Okay," said Frank, and helped his chubby friend into the equipment.

"Isn't anybody coming with me?" Chet asked.

"I'll follow you," said Joe, and started putting on his flippers.

Chet lumbered into the water. As he waddled forward through the shallow surf, Tony snickered.

"That gear makes Chet look like a prehistoric monster!" he said in a low voice.

"Or a frogman from space." Iola giggled.

Chet turned his head, smiled, and waved. He lunged forward and stepped into deeper water.

He should have submerged but his shoulders remained high out of the surf. The young people chuckled.

"Chet's so buoyant he can't go down," said Frank. "Joe, you'd better weigh him down some more. Take an extra lead-filled cartridge belt with you and put it on him."

Joe grabbed the belt and splashed into the surf. Reaching Chet, he attached the extra equipment. Almost at once the stout boy vanished beneath the water. Joe, too, submerged.

Ten minutes later Chet emerged, and swaying from side to side, sloshed to the beach. He removed his face mask and grinned.

"Brought you some souvenirs, girls," he said, and laid a large handful of unusual shells streaked with mother-of-pearl on the sand.

"Oh, they're beautiful!" Callie exclaimed.

Iola clapped Chet on the shoulder. "I'm proud of you, brother. Hope there's a pearl among these."

"How far down did you go?" Tony asked him.

"About twenty feet," Chet stated proudly. "I'll go deeper next time. And here's something else I found."

From one of his belts he brought out what looked like part of a rusty ice pick.

Tony grinned. "I suppose a whale dropped this. He likes his drinks cold and chips off the icebergs with it."

Chet ignored the gibe. "I don't think this is a new ice pick," he retorted. "It's an old one and valuable."

"Sure," said Tony. "It probably belonged to that famous pirate Edward Teach."

"Do you think so?" Chet asked innocently. "I'm going to keep it as a souvenir!"

The picnic group played baseball for twenty minutes, then Frank said, "It seems to me Joe should have come back by this time."

Everyone looked out over the water. Chet scanned the area with the binoculars which Callie had brought ashore in the picnic basket. There was no sign of the diver. Frank became uneasy.

"I'm going to look for Joe," he announced.

Putting on his gear, he hurried into the water and soon was lost to sight. Frank swam up and down the coast off Pirates' Hill but did not see Joe. A sinking feeling came over him. Suppose his brother had been stung by the ray!

Then a more alarming thought struck Frank. He suddenly recalled the black-garbed skin diver who deliberately had aimed a spear at the boys earlier that week. Perhaps the man had returned!

Frank struck out faster and peered around anxiously. Suddenly above him he saw a swimmer whose body extended upright. He was clinging to a boat.

"Joe!" he thought, and hurried toward the figure.

His brother was grasping the gunwale of the *Napoli,* his face mask removed. Frank pulled up alongside of him and removed his.

"Good night!" Frank cried out. "You gave us a scare. Where have you been?"

"Sorry, old man," Joe replied. "I was lying in the bottom of the *Napoli.*"

"Why?" Frank asked in amazement.

"I've been spying on a spy," Joe replied. "Look up to the top of Pirates' Hill! See that figure silhouetted up there? He's been watching every move you've been making on the beach!"

CHAPTER XI

Strange Footprints

"That man's doing more than looking at us," said Frank, staring at the lone figure on the summit of Pirates' Hill. "He's digging!"

From where the Hardys were clinging to the *Napoli,* it certainly looked as if the man were turning up the sand. He held something resembling a blunt shovel.

"He didn't have that before," said Joe. "Maybe he thinks it's safe now for him to dig for whatever he hopes to locate."

"You mean, because we didn't climb the hill?"

"Yes."

"Well, let's climb it now and find out just why he *is* there!" Frank urged. "It's possible he's burying something, not taking it out."

The brothers donned their masks and swam underwater to shore. At once they told the others about the man and the Hardys' desire to see him at close range.

"I suggest that we separate and start looking for driftwood," Frank said. "Then Joe and I will quietly leave the rest of you and sneak up the hill."

The others agreed, promising not to alert the man by looking up. Joe pointed out a circuitous route to the top which would escape the notice of anyone above.

"You take that way, Frank. I'll wander down the beach and go up from another direction. We'll try a pincer movement on the fellow."

"Okay. I wonder if he's Latsky."

"Maybe he's Bowden."

The picnickers began gathering the wood, calling out in loud voices which they hoped would carry to the mysterious man.

"A prize to the one bringing in the most unusual-shaped piece of driftwood," Callie offered.

"Bet I'll win!" Chet yelled.

Minutes later the Hardys were on their separate ways up the dune. They slipped and slid in the heavy sand. Progress was slow, but finally both boys reached the crest. Frank and Joe were about three hundred feet apart as they poked their heads above the top and looked around.

The man was nowhere in sight!

Thinking he might be hiding below a hillock of sand, the Hardys walked toward each other, keeping careful watch. They met without seeing the digger.

"Where'd he go?" Joe asked in disgust. "Do you suppose we scared him off?"

Frank shrugged. "There ought to be footprints. Let's see where they go."

The boys searched and finally found them. The prints were large and far apart, indicating that they had been made by a tall man.

"They go off across the dune in the direction of Sergeant Tilton's house," Frank noted. "But the marks can't be his—he isn't that tall."

The marks might belong to Latsky or Bowden, the brothers decided. Mystified, the boys followed the prints. Suddenly Joe grabbed Frank's arm.

"If it was Latsky, and if he was the one who stole the cutlasses, maybe he was burying them here until the police alert is over."

The boys turned back and dug as best they could with their hands around the area where the stranger had been standing. But nothing came to light.

"Let's go," Joe suggested. "We're giving that man too much of a head start."

The Hardys hurried along the trail of fresh prints in the otherwise smooth sand. The tracks veered suddenly and headed directly for Sergeant Tilton's cottage!

"Maybe we're closing in on the cutlass thief!" said Joe tensely. "This may be his hide-out!"

"You don't mean Tilton?"

"No. But the thief may be boarding with him."

The house, a quaint one-story shingled cottage, stood about three hundred feet away. The dune alternately dipped and rose twice to the high point where the structure was located.

"The footprints lead right to the door!" Frank observed as the boys approached.

Watching to see if anyone might be looking from a window, Frank and Joe walked up and knocked at the door. There was no answer. Frank knocked again. This time someone within stirred. Footsteps sounded and a moment later Sergeant Tilton opened the door.

"Howdy, boys!" he said warmly.

The old artilleryman was dressed in the blue coat and white breeches of an officer in the Revolutionary War, but he had on slippers and was puffing on a battered corncob pipe.

"Well, this seems to be visitors' day around here!" he said, smiling. "Welcome! Come in!"

"Did you have another visitor?" Frank asked, feigning innocence after he had recovered from the surprise of Tilton's appearance.

"Yep. He's gone now."

Sergeant Tilton explained that only a short time before a stranger had stopped at the cottage.

"Where is he now?" Joe asked quickly.

"Oh, he seemed to be in a hurry," Tilton re-

"This may be the thief's hide-out," Joe said tensely

plied. "He was just askin' the best way back to Bayport."

"Who was he?" Joe prodded, trying not to appear too eager to find out.

"Don't rightly know," Tilton answered. "He never said."

"What did he look like?" Frank asked.

"Tall young man. Right nice face. Kind o' greenish eyes an' brown hair. Say, why are you two fellows so all-fired interested in this guy?"

The Hardys laughed. Then Frank told Tilton it was because of their advertisement for information about cannon which the sergeant had answered.

"So if any people are going to dig for it on Pirates' Hill," he added, "Joe and I want to be the ones."

The old man chuckled. "Can't say as I blame you."

Frank now told Sergeant Tilton about Mr. Lightbody's account of the Battle of Bayport. "Do you think there could be any connection between that battle and the cannon you think is buried somewhere up here?"

"I sure do," Tilton replied. "There were some crooked dealin's between those old pirates an' certain folks on land in those days. I figger mebbe somebody ashore was tryin' to sell the cannon or trade it fer the buccaneers' loot."

The artillery sergeant suddenly grinned impishly. "Guess you wonder why I've got this getup on," he said. "I like to dress up in different uniforms. I've got a collection of 'em up in my pirate den. D'you want to see 'em?"

"Pirate den!" Joe exclaimed.

"Yes sirree!" the elderly man replied. "Just follow me."

Though the Hardys felt they should hurry off and try to overtake the young man they wanted to interrogate, they were tempted by Tilton's invitation. Furthermore, they might pick up some valuable information among his treasures.

"All right," said Frank.

Sergeant Tilton led the boys to the kitchen. From an opening in the ceiling hung a rope ladder. The old man grabbed it and thrust his foot into the first rung.

"Up we go!" He laughed. "This is a real genu-wine freebooters' cave I got fer myself up here."

Frank and Joe clambered up after the elderly man, who disappeared into the darkness of the room overhead.

"I'll turn on the lantern," he called. "I made this den out of a storage attic. There's no window. But I couldn't imagine no self-respectin' pirate wantin' a window in his den, anyway."

Tilton switched on a ship's lantern in a corner of the room. The first thing the boys noted in its dim glow was a pair of cutlasses. For a moment they wondered if the weapons could be part of the stolen collection. But just then Tilton blew a cloud of dust off them, in order to show the cutlasses to better advantage. They had definitely been in the den a long time!

"Look at those treasure chests!" Joe cried out. "And all those guns!"

The room contained an amazing collection of corsair relics. Coins, rusted implements, old maps, pirate flags and costumes, and faded oil paintings of famous buccaneers decorated the walls and tables. On a rack in one corner hung a variety of old Army uniforms.

"This is great!" said Joe, and Frank added, "I wish we had time to examine each piece. I'd like to come again, Sergeant Tilton."

"You're welcome any time," the man said.

The boys preceded him down the ladder. As the Hardys were about to leave, the man said, "You know, I plumb forgot to mention something to you. Mebbe it's just my fancy, but it seems kind o' strange at that. The young fellow what was here a little while ago—he's lookin' for a cannon, too!"

"He is!" Frank exclaimed. "Did he say what kind?"

"An old Spanish demiculverin," Tilton replied.

Instantly the brothers' belief that they should talk to the stranger was confirmed. They *must* find him!

"Thanks a lot, Sergeant Tilton," Frank said. "You've been a big help."

"Don't mention it, young fellow," the artillery-man said heartily. "An' hurry back fer a real visit."

Frank and Joe smiled and nodded. Then, following the large footprints that led away from Tilton's cottage, the boys hurried on. The marks led down the side of one dune and up another, but Frank and Joe did not spot their quarry.

At last they reached a point as high as the one on which Tilton's house was situated. Suddenly Joe stopped and gripped Frank's arm. He pointed to a figure in a depression between dunes.

"There's our man!"

CHAPTER XII

A Friendly Suspect

"DON'T let that man get out of sight!" Frank urged, running in a westerly direction through the tall grass on top of the dune.

"He'll have to evaporate to get away this time!" Joe declared, matching his brother step for step. "The fellow's just walking, so we can catch up to him easily."

But they found this to be difficult. He was taking long, fast strides. They ran faster and finally seemed to be closing in on the stranger. He was now in full view, only three hundred yards ahead of them.

"We might call to him," Joe suggested.

"Better not," Frank advised. "If he doesn't want to talk to us, he may run and we'll never catch him."

At this moment the stranger entered the first of a series of deep dips in the sand. The abrupt rise of the knoll between him and the boys blocked the man from view temporarily.

"Oh!" Joe cried out suddenly.

Unfortunately, at that moment, his right foot had slid into a hole in the sand. As he pitched forward, the boy felt a searing pain in his leg.

"Ouch!" Joe cried out. He picked himself up but grimaced.

Frank had turned at his brother's outcry and now came back. "Hard luck," he said. Kneeling beside Joe, he felt the injured ankle joint. "You've sure wrenched it. Better not step on your foot. Lean on me."

"Okay," said Joe. He was annoyed at himself. "That ends our little posse. We can't catch that fellow now."

"Never mind," said Frank. "Put your arm around my shoulder," he suggested. "I'll help you back to the beach and we'll attend to your ankle there."

With Frank helping him, Joe hopped clumsily through the hot sand. In their concern over Joe's ankle, both boys had stopped looking for the man. Now they peered across the wind-swept sand hills, but did not spot him.

"I hate to lose that fellow but it couldn't be helped." Frank sighed.

Moving as fast as Joe's injured ankle would permit, the brothers presently neared the picnic spot. A fire was blazing. The Hardys smiled to see Chet holding two forks in each hand, cooking frankfurters.

"Our friend must have a vacuum for a stomach," Joe remarked. "*Where* does he put so much food?"

Frank did not reply. He was gazing intently at a strange young man who was watching Chet and chatting pleasantly with the girls. The man, about twenty-eight years old, was very tall, and had a determined, jutting jaw. Under his left arm he carried a small canvas sack.

"Joe," said Frank excitedly, "unless my eyes deceive me, the man we were chasing has walked right into our camp!"

"You're right! And carrying his collapsible shovel too."

"One thing's certain," said Frank. "He's not trying to avoid us. But of course he may still be hoping to find out whether we came here to look for a cannon as well as to have a picnic."

"We'd better be cagey!" Joe warned.

As the brothers drew closer, Iola handed the stranger a frankfurter on a roll. A moment later she looked up and saw the Hardys. "Why, Joe, what happened to your foot?" she cried out solicitously and ran toward him.

Joe explained that he had twisted it. He himself was too interested in the stranger to care much about his throbbing ankle.

"I'm sorry you wrenched your ankle," Iola said, adding, "This is Tim Gorman."

"Hi!" said Joe, shaking hands with the easy-mannered stranger.

"And this is Frank Hardy," Iola continued.

Frank, too, shook hands with Gorman, then the brothers exchanged meaningful glances. Tim Gorman was the man who had passed the brothers in a car the day before yesterday and had gazed so intently at them!

The stranger must have guessed their thoughts, for he mentioned the incident before they had a chance. "I was looking for someone who had the same kind of car as yours," he explained. "Sorry I seemed so rude."

Frank and Joe nodded. At the same moment Callie remarked, "Tim Gorman tells us that he has just been to see Mr. Tilton."

"Yes," the visitor said, "I had a very interesting talk with the old artillery sergeant."

"We know that," Frank told him. "We were up there too."

"And I just about broke my leg trying to catch up with you on the dune!" Joe declared. "You certainly crossed it in a hurry."

"Really? Why didn't you call?" Gorman replied. "I didn't see you."

The Hardys' suspicious attitude softened considerably. Gorman now offered to work on Joe's ankle. He made an ice pack with a towel and cubes from the picnic basket, and applied it to the swelling. Next, he massaged the joint carefully. In a few minutes Joe said it felt much better.

"Thanks," he said, as the man rose from the sand.

Frank steered the conversation back to Sergeant Tilton. Gorman talked freely, laughing about the amazing pirate den in the attic and the talkative old man's preposterous stories. But he did not mention the cannon, nor give any inkling of why he had been on Pirates' Hill.

Finally Joe could wait no longer to broach the subject. Bluntly he said, "We understand you're looking for a cannon."

Gorman's face clouded. "I suppose Tilton told you that," he said, his jaw set and his eyes flashing. "That man talks too much. I asked him to keep the information to himself and he told me he would."

"Is it a secret?" Chet asked.

Their visitor looked annoyed, but he regained his composure quickly. "I suppose you might say so," he replied, looking off into space as if trying to decide whether or not to reveal it.

A sudden quiet descended upon the group. The Hardys' friends waited for the brothers to carry on any further conversation.

Tim Gorman relaxed a little and said, "I may

as well admit that I'm looking for a cannon." He paused. "But I'd rather not say anything more about it."

"As you wish," said Frank politely. "But we might be able to help each other. Joe and I have been reading about cannons."

"They sure have," Chet spoke up. "They know a lot about them."

Gorman smiled and said, "That's very interesting. But, after all, we're perfect strangers. I feel it best that I keep my business to myself. Perhaps later on I could discuss the situation with you. For the present I'd prefer not to."

The pleasant way in which he made the latter statement and the smile which went with it tended to disarm all of the group except Frank and Joe. Though Gorman was friendly, they still felt he was somewhat suspect. Not once had he mentioned a demiculverin, though that was, according to Tilton, what he hoped to find. He also did not reveal the contents of the canvas sack.

"We'll probably see one another from time to time," Gorman announced. "I'm staying in Bayport. Perhaps later I'll be in a position to discuss the cannon with you."

The others made no comment. Tony Prito spoke up at this point, however, to ask Gorman if he would like to go back to Bayport with them in the *Napoli*.

"Thanks very much," Gorman answered affably. "But my car is parked over on the shore road."

He started to say good-by to the picnickers, then suddenly he stopped short and stared at an object in Iola's hand. It was the ice pick Chet had found. She was about to put it into the picnic basket.

Gorman stepped forward. "Where did you get that?" he asked intently.

Chet proudly informed Gorman of his underwater discovery as Iola handed over the pick. Gorman examined it closely.

"Is it an antique ice pick?" Chet asked him.

Gorman swung about, his face flushed with excitement. "This is not an ice pick. It's a gunner's pick! There *was* a cannon near here!"

CHAPTER XIII

Overboard!

TIM GORMAN's announcement sent a thrill of excitement through the Hardy boys. There was no question now that a cannon had been on Pirates' Hill. But what was more important, was it still buried deep under the sand? Or had the old cannon by this time been washed into the sea?

Frank was the first to speak. "Have you any idea, Tim, what kind of cannon it might have been?"

The Hardys waited impatiently for the young man's answer, but they were disappointed in it. "There's absolutely no way of telling," he replied slowly.

The brothers wondered if it could have been a demiculverin. They did not mention this, however.

Chet had walked up to face their visitor. "How

did you know this gadget was really a gunner's pick?" he asked.

"Like Frank and Joe, I've been reading a good deal about artillery," the young man replied. He turned the pick over in his hands and continued, "This is part of an eighteenth-century gunner's equipment. It's one of eleven important tools a gunner needed."

"How was this pick used?" Chet inquired.

Gorman explained that by the eighteenth century, powder bags had come into wide use, replacing the loose powder which had formerly been ladled into the bore of a cannon.

"This made it necessary to prick open the bag so the priming fire from the vent could reach the charge."

"Then what?" Chet asked expectantly.

"That's where the gunner's pick came in. It was plunged into the vent far enough to pierce the bag. It's sometimes called a priming wire."

Callie suddenly chuckled. "It sounds complicated to me. I'd need several lessons to get this through my head."

"I would too," Iola confessed.

Gorman smiled. "I'll be glad to give you girls cannon instruction any time you say."

Chet and Tony chuckled, but Frank and Joe Hardy shot the man dark looks. They did not want their friends making dates with any person who was a suspect!

Callie and Iola guessed the boys' thoughts. To tease them, Iola said, "We'll let you know, Tim."

"Don't forget," Gorman said, grinning. "Well, I must be off now."

He shook hands with everyone and said good-by. When he was out of sight, the boys discussed the man's contradictory manner.

The girls did not agree with the boys. "I think he's charming," said Iola.

Callie added, winking at her friend, "And so good looking. But you boys needn't be jealous," she added impishly.

"Who's jealous?" Joe stormed.

The girls giggled. Then they became serious and all discussed the possibility of the demicul verin being hidden on Pirates' Hill.

"You'd better dig for it pretty soon or Gorman will find it first," Callie advised.

"Let's start right now," Frank urged.

Acting as leader he assigned the others to various spots and for an hour the beach and hillside were beehives of activity. Various small objects were dug up but there was no sign of a cannon.

"I guess we'll have to quit!" Tony called out to Frank. He explained that he had promised to be home for supper by seven and take his parents in the *Napoli* later to see the fireworks.

"We're all going to see them," said Iola. "Sorry you can't join us, Tony."

The tools were collected and carried out to the

boat along with the picnic baskets. After everyone was seated, Tony headed back toward town. Frank and Joe sat alone in the prow for a while discussing Gorman. Frank said he was convinced the young man was aboveboard, but Joe was still suspicious.

"He may just be a very smooth operator," Joe remarked. "Why, he might even be in league with Latsky!"

"What gives you that idea?" Frank asked his brother.

"He certainly knows a lot about the history of ancient artillery."

The boys were interrupted in their discussion by a call from Callie. "Oh, look, everybody!"

The *Napoli* had turned into the bay and was running close to shore where an area of the water had been roped off for the evening's display of fireworks. A small grandstand had been erected along the bank. In the water two large scows contained the set pieces and the rockets which would be sent skyward in the evening's celebration.

"Looks as if it'll be a good show," Tony remarked.

Chet proposed that his group come early in the *Sleuth* and anchor as close as possible to the two barges so they could get an excellent view of the performance.

"Suppose we meet at the dock at eight-thirty,"

Frank suggested. "The fireworks start at nine."

This was agreed upon. Iola suggested that when they arrived in Bayport they transfer the picnic baskets to the *Sleuth* and use the food that was left for a late snack.

"That's using your head, Sis," Chet said approvingly.

Iola had stood up to see the set pieces of fireworks. As Tony steered back to the center of the bay, she sat down on the gunwale of the boat. She began to croon, "Sailing, sailing over the bounding main," and the others joined in.

When the song ended, Frank sang lustily, "Oh, my name was Captain Brand, a-sailing—"

Suddenly the *Napoli* hit something in the water. The boat gave an abrupt lurch, causing Iola to lose her balance. She fell, banging her head on the gunwale, then toppled into the water.

"Oh!" Callie screamed. "She's hurt!"

Everyone jumped up as the boat rocked dangerously. Instantly Joe kicked off his loafers and dived overboard as Iola disappeared under the waves thirty feet astern of the *Napoli*. With strong strokes Joe reached the spot and surface-dived, while Tony circled the boat back at reduced speed.

As the group watched with worried expressions, Joe's head popped to the surface for a second. He sucked in air, then went under again.

Without a word to his companions, Frank quickly donned his skin-diving gear and was about to plunge over the side when his brother appeared again. This time he had an arm around the girl.

Iola Morton was limp. Apparently she had been knocked unconscious before falling into the water.

Ready hands pulled her aboard and Chet at once applied first aid. There were a few anxious moments on everyone's part before Iola's eyelids flickered open and she began to breathe normally. Frank told her what had happened.

"You sure you feel okay?" Chet asked solicitously.

"Yes—thanks to you and Joe," Iola said gratefully.

As soon as Tony was sure Iola was all right, he dived overboard to inspect his craft. Fortunately it had not been damaged by a log which had hit it and was now floating nearby. He climbed aboard and reported this to the others.

"It was a close squeak," Joe remarked.

As the *Napoli* proceeded to the Hardys' dock, Iola insisted that she felt fine. But she did promise to go home at once and rest until it was time to attend the fireworks display.

Upon reaching the dock, Chet transferred the picnic baskets to the *Sleuth*. Then the Hardys, the Mortons, and Callie said good-by to Tony and drove off. They went directly to the Mortons'.

At eight-thirty Frank and Joe drove their mother and aunt over to some friends with whom they were to attend the fireworks display and spend the evening. Then the boys went to their dock where Chet and the girls were waiting. Soon the group was aboard the *Sleuth*, heading out to the area where the fireworks were to be displayed. Nearing it, they could hear spine-tingling band music from the grandstand on the shore.

A large crowd was gathered both on the bank and on the water. Small craft filled with onlookers bustled in the harbor, each skipper seeking a good place from which to view the fireworks.

Frank guided the *Sleuth* close to the roped-off area. Floodlights set up on the scows made the scene as bright as day.

As Frank turned off his motor, Joe, seated alongside him, suddenly grabbed his brother's arm.

"What's up?" Frank asked, turning. He noticed a worried look on his brother's face.

"The man who seems to be in charge of the fireworks display is the one who warned us about the sting ray!"

Frank gazed ahead and nodded. "I wonder if the fellow who was hiding in the bottom of his boat is here too."

There was no possible way to find out now. It

was two minutes to nine. The man in charge was hastily directing several workers, none of whom was familiar to the boys.

"They're going to start!" Chet called.

A moment later there was a swish and whine as the first rocket was set off. It shot high into the dark sky above the harbor and a fountain of cascading diamonds burst into life. Ohs and ahs echoed from the onlookers.

A second and a third rocket swirled heavenward. Red and blue sparkles gleamed brilliantly after the sharp explosions.

"This is wonderful!" Iola cried out.

"Oh, they're going to set off one of the figures!" Callie said excitedly. "Look, it's a man pedaling a bicycle!"

A twenty-foot figure, sputtering a yellow-white smoke, appeared to be cycling across the barge.

"There goes another figure!" Chet cried in delight as a multicolored clown began to dance with slow, jerky motions.

Just then a hissing sound attracted the attention of the Hardys and their friends. The next moment a terrified shriek went up from the girls.

A rocket had been fired horizontally and was streaking directly toward the *Sleuth!*

CHAPTER XIV

The Elusive Mr. X

TERRIFIED, everyone in the *Sleuth* sprawled flat, as the rocket skittered over the waves like a guided missile!

Whack! A shudder went through the boat as the rocket glanced off her bow. A thundering blast followed when the missile exploded ten yards off the starboard side.

Streamers of white light ribboned across the motorboat, but the hot rocket itself sizzled on the surface of the water and then died out in a cloud of acrid smoke.

"That was too close for comfort!" Joe cried out, jumping up.

Frank leaped back to the wheel as Chet, Iola, and Callie sat up and peered over the gunwales toward the barge.

"That was no accident!" Frank stormed. "I'm going after the man who set off the rocket!"

"Pour it on!" Joe shouted.

107

The motor roared to life and the propeller kicked up white foam as the *Sleuth* shot ahead and ducked under the rope of the danger zone.

Closing in rapidly on the barge, the Hardys noticed that one of the Bayport Police Department launches was approaching from the opposite side. Its two powerful spotlights were raking the fireworks platform and the officers were shouting that there was to be no more firing.

"Look!" Joe cried. "That one man isn't paying any attention!"

A stranger to the Hardys, he grabbed a lighted torch from the hands of the head man and started for one of the rockets.

"He'll blow us all up!" Callie cried in terror.

A second later the young people saw him run from fixture to fixture, touching his torch to the fuses of the entire remaining display.

Frank did not wait. He put the *Sleuth* in reverse, and the motorboat skittered backward.

The next moment, the bay shook with the din of the bursting pyrotechnics. Rockets spewed in all directions with thunderous detonations.

The danger of being struck by the flying rockets also drove the police launch back from the barge toward the center of the bay. There were anxious moments as the bombardment continued.

Hot fragments from the bursting rockets sprayed the deck and cockpit of the *Sleuth,* but finally Frank got beyond their range.

The din aboard the barge ended as abruptly as it had begun. One glowing wheel continued to turn slowly, but the rockets had spent themselves.

"What a crazy, stupid thing to do!" Joe exclaimed.

"Thank goodness we're all right!" said Callie. "Frank, you're a wonder!"

"I'm nothing of the sort," the boy replied, "and I'd like to punch the guy who set off those rockets."

"You'll have a hard time," Chet declared. "All the men on the barges jumped overboard and are swimming to shore."

"I can try!" Frank declared.

He turned the boat and headed for the beach. The stranger who had caused the uproar was not in sight, but the man who had warned them of the sting ray was still in the water. Frank drew alongside of him and throttled the engine.

"Climb in!" he called.

The man pulled himself aboard. At the same time the police launch picked up several other swimmers. Not one of them was the man the Hardys wanted to interrogate. But they began to question their own new passenger.

"Who was the man who started that explosion?" Joe demanded.

"I don't know."

"What do you mean? You were in charge of the fireworks, weren't you, Mr—er?"

The man scowled. "The name's Halpen. I was only in charge of the timing," he answered. "The fellows lighted the fuses when I told 'em to. I don't know the name of the guy who disobeyed orders. He just came around before we were ready to start, and I supposed somebody had hired him. It wasn't any of my business."

Frank was not satisfied with the explanation. He hailed the captain of the police boat and asked if he might speak to the men they had picked up.

"Sure thing, Frank," said the officer.

He requested the men to come to the near side of his craft. Frank asked them the name of the worker who had set off the rockets. Each declared he did not know.

Their own passenger grunted. "I guess the guy just butted in for a good time," he remarked. He eyed the Hardys. "Unless," he went on, "the man was an enemy of yours."

"If he was, we didn't know it," Joe retorted quickly. "But he sure is now. He's in for a lot of explaining when we catch up with him!"

At the moment there seemed little possibility of this. The man had disappeared and the boys assumed he had swum up the shore line and come out on the beach some distance beyond the crowd.

"I'm getting cold," said Halpen. "Put me ashore, will you?"

"Okay, but first I want to ask you a few questions," Joe spoke up.

"Well, make it snappy!"

"Who was the man hidden under the tarpaulin in your boat the other day?" Joe shot at him.

Halpen's jaw sagged, his composure gone completely. He did not answer at once. When he did, the boys felt sure that the man was not telling the truth.

"So you saw him, eh? You got good eyesight. Well, he was a stranger to me. His boat capsized and I picked him up. He didn't tell me his name."

"But why did he hide under the tarpaulin?" Joe persisted.

"Afraid of the sun," Halpen answered bluntly. "And he fell asleep."

Frank took up the questioning. "Why did you race off in your speedboat when we tried to overtake you?"

Halpen glared at the boy. "You're a wise guy, aren't you? I wasn't running away or that stranger, either. It was late. My wife was waiting for me. And now, take me to a boat so I can get to my car."

The Hardys felt frustrated, but there was nothing more they could do. Frank let the man off, then proceeded toward his own dock.

Iola grimaced. "I don't believe one word that man said, do you?"

There was a chorus of "No's." Joe said he was going to find out who Halpen was and what he did for a living.

"I'll bet it's nothing much," Chet spoke up, opening one of the picnic baskets. "Who wants a sandwich and some soda?"

Everyone did and in a short while all the food had been consumed. Chet declared that he was still hungry, so upon reaching the Hardy dock, the group set off for a spot frequented by teen-agers which bore a sign:

Bill's Burgers
Biggest on the Bay

Immediately the Hardys' friends went to phone their families that they were all right. Then Joe called the chairman of the fireworks committee, Mr. Atkin. He had just reached home.

"Halpen's harmless but a ne'er-do-well," Atkin said in answer to Joe's question. "He manages to get along somehow, doing odd jobs. At one time he worked in a pyrotechnics factory and under-stands fireworks. Halpen's had the job of setting off the Bayport rockets and set pieces for the last several years. I can't understand what happened tonight."

"It scared the wits out of us," said Joe, then asked if Halpen owned a speedboat.

"Oh, no. But he manages to borrow boats from people he knows."

Joe now inquired how many men had been en-gaged to set off the fireworks display.

"Let's see," said Mr. Atkin. "Five. Yes, there were five."

"I counted six," the boy told him.

"What!" the man exclaimed. "Then one of them was there without being hired. He probably was the one who caused a near tragedy."

"I'm sure the mysterious Mr. X was the culprit," Joe agreed. Returning to the group, he told the others that so far Halpen's story checked. "It's a puzzle, though. I have a hunch the man's not to be trusted."

Frank remarked that he was more worried about the mysterious man who seemed to have aimed a rocket at them.

"You think he did it on purpose!" Callie exclaimed fearfully. "But why? He couldn't have known we'd be there."

"Of course not," Frank agreed. "But when he did spot us, he grabbed the opportunity."

Chet leaned across the table, his eyes bulging. "You mean that guy's mixed up with the cannon gang and wanted to bump us off?"

"It's hard to decide," Frank replied.

The thought of their close escape from possible death sobered the group. It was not until some of their high school friends stopped at the table and began to joke with them that they pulled themselves out of the depressed mood.

It was midnight when Frank and Joe returned

home. Mrs. Hardy and Aunt Gertrude were worriedly awaiting them.

"We saw the wild ending of the fireworks display and have been disturbed ever since," said the boys' mother, "even though we called the Mortons and learned no one was hurt. Thank goodness you're really all right."

"But no credit to you two," Aunt Gertrude spoke up tartly. "It's shameful the way you always manage to get in the way of danger. If I were your mother—"

"But, Aunty, we're here in one piece, so what's the difference," Joe interrupted. "Now if we had come walking in here minus our heads—!"

"Oh, stop your nonsense!" their aunt ordered. She turned on her heel and started up the stairs, calling, "Good night, everyone. You'd all better get some sleep."

The next morning, while the boys were dressing, Frank said he thought they should get in touch with Bowden before making a further search. "Since both he and Tim Gorman are looking for the demiculverin, I'd like to know if they're acquainted."

"Let's go!"

"We'll tell him Chet found a gunner's pick along the shore, but we won't mention Pirates' Hill."

"Right."

After breakfast the boys phoned Bowden at his motel and asked if they might call on him. "Sure, come on over," he replied. "I'll be waiting for you."

The man seemed a bit less friendly than usual when they arrived. Was he suspicious of them? But when the boys had told their story, he smiled. "You're making progress, I can see that. Keep it up. Time is precious."

Bowden had nothing to offer in the way of news. The police, he said, had no clues to the person who had left him the warning note and later attacked him.

Presently Frank asked, "Do you know a man named Tim Gorman?"

Bowden was visibly disturbed by the question. "Gorman!" he exclaimed, his face flushing. "I'll say I know him, but I'm not proud of it."

"What do you mean?" Joe asked.

"He's no good!" Bowden told the boys that Gorman went about posing as a naval man and was wanted by the police for swindling.

"That's hard to believe," Frank said.

Joe, on the other hand, arched his eyebrows and gave his brother a meaningful look, as if to say, "I told you so."

Bowden asked the boys how they happened to know Gorman. Guardedly Frank told of meeting him on the beach. Bowden listened intently. He interrupted the narration several times to ask about details. There seemed to be something he wanted to know, but would not ask point-blank.

Finally, unable to contain himself any longer, he blurted out, "Did Gorman mention the cutlass?"

CHAPTER XV

An Alias

BOWDEN's unexpected question caught Joe off guard. Instead of giving a counter query which might have netted the boys some valuable information, he asked bluntly, "One of the stolen cutlasses?"

Joe's thoughtless remark made Frank wince, and his brother immediately realized his mistake. Their father certainly would not approve of such careless detective work! If Bowden had anything to hide concerning the stolen cutlasses, he now was forewarned.

"Stolen? No, of course not," the man said flatly.

"Then what cutlass are you talking about?"

"Forget it."

Joe, annoyed at his own blunder and Bowden's reluctance to talk, said grimly, "Mr. Bowden, we can't have you playing hide-and-seek with facts and still do a good sleuthing job for you."

The man smiled patronizingly. "No need for you to get hot under the collar. Gorman's hipped on finding a miniature cutlass—says it's a lost heirloom or something of the sort. He puts the question to any new acquaintance."

The Hardys felt this was an unlikely story. "Are you sure?" Frank asked.

"Positive. But he may pretend it's a real one just for effect. Gorman's not given to telling the truth."

Frank and Joe suppressed smiles at this remark. Neither was Bowden noted for sticking to the facts!

The boys left shortly, saying they planned to continue their search for the cannon. Bowden waved good-by from the motel entrance, urging them to speed up their work.

"I wish Dad would hurry back from Florida," Frank remarked, as they rode along. "This case is getting knotty."

Joe nodded. "It sure is—as knotty as a pine board!"

Frank grinned. "I wish we could look through one of those knots and see the answer." Then, after a few moments, he added thoughtfully, "Joe, this case had me baffled until just now. But I believe I have the answer."

"What is it?"

"It might sound farfetched," Frank replied, as the car hummed closer to Bayport, "but the combination of cannons, cutlasses, and the story about the pirates' fight all lead in one direction."

Joe smiled. "I get it. You mean hidden treasure."

"Right."

His brother's face broke into a wide grin. "If there's treasure around this territory, let's locate it!" he said with enthusiasm.

"We'll have to dig up more clues, though, before we can dig up any treasure," Frank said.

Since the boys had to go near their home to take the road to Pirates' Hill, Frank suggested that they stop and see if there was a letter or phone message from Mr. Hardy. He turned onto Elm Street and pulled into their driveway.

The Hardy telephone was ringing persistently as the brothers entered the house. "Nobody's home," Frank said. "Grab it, Joe."

The boy picked up the instrument in the front hall. "Yes. This is Joe Hardy. . . . Who? I didn't get the last name. . . . Oh, Smedick. Why do you want to see us, Mr. Smedick?" Joe listened for a moment and added, "All right. Frank and I will come immediately."

Joe hung up and turned to his brother. "A guy with a strained voice, named A. B. Smedick, wants to see us at the Bayport Hotel. Room 309. It has something to do with the cannon mystery. Let's go!"

"Who is he?" Frank asked cautiously.

"He didn't explain."

"We'd better watch out. This may be a trap. I suggest we stay in the hall and talk to this fellow."

Frank left a note for his mother telling of their change in plans. A few minutes later the boys parked their convertible in a lot alongside the hotel. The elevator in the lobby took them to the third floor and the young sleuths stepped out. Joe buzzed 309 and the boys waited. Presently the door opened. The brothers gasped. Tim Gorman stood there!

"What's the idea of this?" Joe asked.

"Please step in," Gorman invited. "I'll explain."

"We prefer staying here," said Frank coolly.

Quickly Gorman reached into his coat pocket, extracted a wallet, and took out a paper and a card. He handed them to Frank.

"This one is my honorable discharge from the Navy," Gorman said, "and the other my naval identification card."

On the card the boys saw the small photograph of the man in a Navy uniform. Joe inspected it closely to see if any touching up had been done.

It was Gorman, all right, beyond any doubt. The paper was a statement of the man's honorable discharge from the United States Navy two years earlier.

"Please come in," Gorman said, and the brothers entered the room. Their host locked the door and they all sat down close together.

"I'm using the name of Smedick here for protection against certain people in Bayport who would like to see me harmed. They know me by name only."

Without explaining further, he went on, "I've investigated you boys thoroughly and know you're trustworthy. I'm very eager to have you help me solve a mystery."

"We're pretty busy right now on another case," said Joe, who still felt skeptical about the man.

Gorman looked disappointed. "I'm sorry to hear that. I really need your help."

Frank suggested that Gorman tell them what the mystery was. Perhaps they could work on it along with their other sleuthing.

Fully expecting to hear that the man was looking for a demiculverin on Pirates' Hill, the brothers were surprised when Gorman pulled a pad and pencil from his pocket and wrote:

Meet me tomorrow at 2 P.M. in the brown shack on the dune a mile north of Pirates' Hill. I'll tell you then.

The boys read the message. Frank nodded but Joe, suspicious, took the pad and wrote:

How do we know this isn't some kind of trap?

Gorman seemed disturbed by the boys' lack of faith in him. But he smiled at the Hardys and wrote a note suggesting that they use the word Collado—the name of a Spanish artillery expert of 1592—as a challenge, and, for a countersign, the name of Hotchkiss, an American artillery expert.

Joe looked annoyed. "How many people will know about this?" he asked aloud. "And before we go any further, suppose you tell us what you know about cutlasses."

The boy's remark hit Gorman like a bombshell. He sat bolt upright in his chair, and his face flushed. "Please, not now," he said in a strained voice. "Tomorrow. I'll tell you then. I'll be waiting for you."

He arose, took a lighter from his pocket, and burned the notes. Then Gorman walked to the door, unlocked it, and ushered the boys out.

"I'll see you tomorrow," he said, closing the door.

The Hardys did not speak until they reached their car. Then, as they drove off, Joe burst out, "What do you make of all this?"

Frank said his curiosity was aroused and he would like to go to the cabin. "But I'll watch out for any double-crossing."

Joe declared he was going to check with the Navy Department in an effort to learn what Gorman had been doing since his discharge. "Do you realize he didn't tell us, Frank, and the man could have become a real phony since that time?"

"You're right. But I doubt that the Navy Department can give you much help on that score."

Nevertheless, he turned toward their house so Joe could put in a phone call to Washington and make his request to an officer. He made the connection, but the answer, though polite, was discouraging.

"It takes us some time to make a check once a man has been discharged. It might take weeks."

Joe thanked the officer and hung up. "You were right, Frank," he admitted. "I guess we'll have to carry on without the information. Well, let's get started for Pirates' Hill."

"Let's borrow Dad's magnetometer," Joe added. This was an electronic mine detector for locating metals under sand. "Shall we drive or take the *Sleuth?*"

"Both," his brother answered. "This gear is heavy. Let's drive to our dock and go on by boat."

Once more Frank left a note for Mrs. Hardy, while Joe got the magnetometer, then they drove off in the convertible. Joe, thoughtful a few minutes, said, "Frank, we might even unearth the pirate treasure if there is one!"

"Sure," his brother said, grinning. "But we'd better stick to looking for the demiculverin."

The day was overcast and the brothers found the bay fairly choppy. Frank tied a rowboat to the stern to avoid wading ashore with all their gear. By the time Joe anchored the *Sleuth* off Pirates' Hill, a rough surf was churning onto the beach and the rock ledges.

"Let's do our searching systematically," Frank said. He proposed that they mark off sectors and work along the beach and the dunes, moving slowly up the hill.

They worked steadily until one o'clock. The magnetometer had indicated nothing of importance. The boys sat down to rest and eat the sandwiches they had brought. It was ebb tide and the beach was deserted.

Suddenly Joe began to laugh. "Look at those crows getting a free lunch!"

A dozen of the big black birds were digging up clams. The boys watched in fascination as the crows hopped along the wet sand and nipped at the extended necks of unwary victims. Frank and Joe chuckled as the solemn birds wiggled their necks, trying to pry the stubborn clams from their homes.

Finally one would yield and the crow would fly high, drop the clam on a rock to crack the shell, then eat the juicy contents.

"Pretty tough on the clam," Frank remarked.

As soon as he and Joe had finished eating, they resumed their work with the magnetometer. Whenever it indicated a metal object under the sand, the boys dug hopefully. As time passed they discovered a battered watch, a charm bracelet and a dime-store ring, along with a tobacco tin and an old, rusty anchor.

"Say, we could open a secondhand store," Joe quipped.

"And a junk yard, too."

By five o'clock the beach and part of the hill were full of excavations but the boys had not found any artillery. Unfortunately, the magnetometer short-circuited. It would take some time to repair it, they knew. Weary, they gave up the search.

"At this rate it'll take us all summer to cover Pirates' Hill," Frank remarked, flopping down on the sand to rest.

"Yes, and Bowden's in a hurry," Joe answered with a grin.

They rowed back to the *Sleuth* and started homeward. Soon after supper the Hardy phone rang. It was Chief Collig calling the boys.

"I have some important news for you," he told Frank, who had answered.

"What's up, Chief?"

"First, I want to tell you that we still have the stakeout posted at the cabin in the woods, but no one has showed up yet."

"Too bad," said Frank.

"That's not the only thing I called you up about, though. The department has been working on the fireworks case. Since you fellows are interested in finding that phony helper I thought you'd like to know we've traced him to a rooming house."

"Where?" Frank asked.

"Right here in Bayport. His name is Guiness. He skipped out just before we got there, but we picked up a clue that may help us locate him. Patrolman Smuff found it in a wastebasket in Guiness's room."

Frank gripped the phone excitedly. "What is it?"

"An address on a scrap of paper," the chief replied. "It reads *A. B. Smedick, B. H.*"

CHAPTER XVI

A Surprising Search

STUNNED by the information, Frank echoed in amazement, "A. B. Smedick, B. H.!"

"Right," said the police chief. "What do you think B. H. stands for?"

"I'm sure that it means Bayport Hotel," Frank replied, "because we talked to a person there by that name."

"What! Well, then, maybe you can tell us where Smedick is now. He checked out."

Frank, amazed to hear this, said he had no idea. "Joe and I are supposed to meet him tomorrow afternoon along the shore. He probably won't show up. But if he does, I'll try to find out if he knows where Guiness is."

"Do that," said Chief Collig and hung up.

As soon as Frank replaced the phone in its cradle, he rushed to tell Joe, his mother, and Aunt Gertrude the news.

"That man who tried to blow us up is either an enemy or a friend of Gorman or Smedick or whatever our Navy man's name is," Frank reeled off in a single breath. He related quickly the message from Chief Collig.

"It sounds to me," Aunt Gertrude commented, her jaw set firmly, "as if everybody connected with this Pirates' Hill mystery is a criminal. It's high time you quit the case."

"And not apprehend any of them?" Joe protested. "Oh, Aunty, we can't stop now!"

"Dad will be disappointed in us if we don't solve this mystery," Frank added. He turned to Joe. "At this point I can almost share your suspicions about Gorman."

Joe gave a knowing grin. "I thought you'd agree sooner or later, but it took the police to convince you."

"Hold on! I didn't say I'm entirely convinced. I'll let you know after we talk to Gorman at that shack tomorrow afternoon."

"If he shows up," Joe added.

Next morning, when the Hardys awoke, a heavy rain was falling. Jumping out of bed to close the window, Frank remarked, "No wonder the bay was kicking up yesterday. This storm was on its way then. It doesn't look as if we'll be able to do any searching at Pirates' Hill today."

During breakfast the boys decided to spend the forenoon doing some sleuthing on the stolen cutlasses. Perhaps they would provide an important clue.

"There's a good chance that they may have turned up at some of the curio shops and pawnbrokers by this time," Frank observed. "Let's make the rounds of those places as a starter."

The boys' first stop was a curio shop near the Bayport railroad station. The owner lived alone in two rooms in the rear of the store. Frank gave the old-fashioned bellpull several tugs. A few moments went by before the proprietor appeared at the door. There was soap lather on his chin.

"Step right in, boys," he said eagerly. "You're early. Just look around while I finish shaving." He returned to the back room.

"This man has got a lot of interesting-looking weapons," Frank said presently, after walking around. He eyed an old-time flintlock hanging on the wall. "But," he added, "none of them has any special mark such as the authentic pieces have. These must all be imitations."

"Shall we leave?" Joe asked his brother. "We're probably wasting our time."

Though his voice was low, it carried to the rear of the shop. The proprietor came running out, pleading with the boys not to go until he had shown them the weapons.

"Sorry, we're looking for antique cutlasses," Frank told him.

"What difference does the age make," the man

asked, "if you want a cutlass? If you don't have much money, I can rent you a sword."

Joe grinned. "Tell you what. If you can rent me a white Arabian horse along with the cutlass, it's a deal."

The dealer, realizing that he had been trying a little too hard to make customers of them, smiled and told the boys to come back some other time.

"Well, score zero for us on that call." Joe sighed as they climbed into their car.

The Hardys drove across town to a shabby antique shop, owned and operated by a Mr. Dumian.

"Yes, I have cutlasses," the dealer replied to Frank's question. He eyed the boys with curiosity over his bifocal glasses. "It's funny you're wanting them. A short time ago a boy named Gil Fanning—about eighteen years old—brought five cutlasses in here to sell. Told me they were family relics."

"Is he a local boy?" Frank asked, interested at once.

"Yes. He lives in Bayport," Mr. Dumian answered. "On Central Avenue. I paid him twenty dollars apiece—a pretty steep price, but they were the real thing. Beautiful cutlasses."

"May we see them?" Frank asked eagerly. The thought that they might be the Entwistle relics caused his heart to beat faster.

"I'm sorry," the dealer replied. "Right after Fanning brought the weapons in, a swarthy-looking fellow in a black motorcycle jacket came into the shop and bought every one!"

The Hardys shot chagrined looks at each other. It appeared that Latsky had beat them to the draw! Furthermore, the Hardys were dumfounded by the appearance of Latsky at the shop —assuming that the man in the leather jacket was he. It certainly looked now as if Latsky were not the person who had taken the cutlasses from the Historical Society's building. Could Gil Fanning have been the thief?

"That's not all," the man continued. "Last evening, just as I was closing up shop, a stout boy came in here looking for cutlasses. And now when you fellows come in asking for the same thing, I begin to wonder if there—"

"Did this stout fellow give his name?" Joe broke in.

"Yes," Mr. Dumian said, turning to a spindle of notes on his desk. "He wanted me to get in touch with him if any more cutlasses came in. Here it is." He tore a slip of paper off the spindle and handed it to Frank.

The paper bore the name Chet Morton!

"Chet Morton! We know him," Joe burst out. "What would he want with the swords?"

"Search me," said Mr. Dumian.

The boys thanked him and left the shop. Once

outside, they decided to talk to Gil Fanning, then ride out to Chet's house and ask him why he was looking for cutlasses.

"What a muddle!" Frank exclaimed, as the brothers went into a drugstore to look up the name Fanning in the Bayport telephone directory. One was listed at 70 Central Avenue.

Frank and Joe drove there in the downpour and found that Gil, an orphan, lived with his grandparents. Tearfully the elderly woman said the boy had not been home for a week.

"He's always been hard to manage," she said, "but we knew where he was. This is the first time he's ever stayed away without letting us hear where he is."

"Have you notified the police?" Frank asked.

"Oh, no," Mrs. Fanning replied. "Gil phoned he'd be back in a while—had a job. We were not to worry." Suddenly she asked, "But why are you here? Is our boy in some kind of trouble?"

"Not that we know of," Frank answered. "Mrs. Fanning, did you give Gil permission to sell any of your heirlooms?"

"Cutlasses," Joe added.

A frightened look came over the woman's face. "You mean swords? We never had any swords. You must be mistaken."

"No doubt." Frank smiled, not wishing to disturb the elderly woman any further. "Well, thank you," he said. "I hope Gil returns soon."

Frank and Joe left, puzzled by the information. Where was Gil Fanning?

The rain was coming down in torrents now. Driving carefully as water gushed off the windshield with each sweep of the wipers, Frank headed for Chet Morton's. Presently he came to a sharp bend in the road.

"Better slow down," Joe advised. "This is like a hurricane!"

Hugging the right side of the highway, the boys suddenly heard and saw through the torrential rain an automobile racing into the curve from the opposite direction. It swung awkwardly and went into a skid, then sped almost side-on toward the Hardys' car!

"Look out!" Joe yelled.

Frank swung to avoid a collision. But in doing so, the convertible veered toward a deep ditch!

CHAPTER XVII

A Missing Pal

THE brothers felt a terrific lurch as the wheels on the right side of the car dropped into the soft, rain-soaked ditch. The convertible tilted dangerously, and Frank fought hard to get it back on the road.

Just when it seemed as if the car could not possibly stay upright, the mired front wheel leaped onto the hard surface. Then the rear one pulled up.

"Golly!" Joe exclaimed. "I thought we were goners!"

Frank heaved a sigh, then muttered angrily, "That crazy driver ought to have his license revoked!" He hopped out to inspect the wheels, but no damage had been done.

As he started off again, Joe said, "Say, do you suppose he tried to force us into the ditch on purpose, hoping we'd overturn?"

"You mean the driver was one of our enemies?" Frank smiled ruefully. "If he was trying to cause an accident, he nearly accomplished his purpose."

As they neared the Morton farm, the rain ended but the landscape was dotted with huge puddles. Trees and bushes sagged under the heavy weight of water.

On reaching the farmhouse, Frank and Joe learned from Iola that about an hour ago Chet had taken his flippers and snorkel, and gone to their swimming pool to practice skin diving.

"Chet's still talking about buying an outfit like you boys have," said his sister. She smiled. "He says he can't earn enough money for it by working on the farm, so he's going to look for another job."

Frank and Joe chuckled. Their stout friend had never displayed any interest in work. Over a period of years Chet had had to be cajoled by his family and the Hardys to finish jobs he had started. Seldom had he been known to look for work!

"Chet sure must want that diving equipment bad," Joe remarked.

Iola said her brother was intensely interested in skin diving. "Ever since he found that gunner's pick, he's had a great desire to dive for treasure."

Frank and Joe told Iola about their search the

day before, then went to the pool to talk to Chet about his visit to the antique store. They wanted to know why he was looking for cutlasses.

To their surprise, Chet was not in sight. At the edge of the pool lay his snorkel and flippers. The Hardys walked around the pool, peering down into the water. Chet was not there.

"He must be off earning some money," said Joe with a grin.

The brothers returned to the farmhouse and told Mrs. Morton and Iola that Chet was not around. Both looked concerned. Mrs. Morton said that Chet never left the farm without saying where he was going.

"Perhaps he went off with that boy who was here," Iola suggested. She told the Hardys that about half an hour ago a youth about Chet's age had strolled in and asked for him. They had directed him to the pool.

"Who was he?" Frank asked.

"We'd never seen him before," Iola answered. "He said his name was Gil. He didn't give his last name."

At this announcement Frank and Joe stared questioningly at each other. Was he Gil Fanning, the boy who had brought the cutlasses to Mr. Dumian's shop to sell?

"What's the matter?" asked Iola, noting the boys' puzzled expressions.

Frank told her and Mrs. Morton the whole

story. Both of them looked worried and Mrs. Morton said, "Oh, dear, I hope nothing will happen to Chet!"

Frank and Joe tried to reassure her that he knew how to take care of himself, but secretly they, too, were greatly worried.

"If the boys went off together walking, they probably haven't gone far," said Frank. "We didn't pass them on the road, so they must have headed in the other direction. We're driving that way, Mrs. Morton, so we'll look for Chet."

"If you don't find him, will you please telephone?" Mrs. Morton requested. "If Chet isn't home within an hour, or if I don't hear from him, I'm going to call the police."

The Hardys hurried off. As they rode along, their eyes constantly swept the landscape, hoping to catch sight of their chum. They went for three miles without passing a car or seeing anyone walking along the road. Presently they came to a combination country store and gasoline station.

"I'll go in and phone," said Frank, getting out of the car.

Joe decided to go along, eager to learn any news of Chet. The Hardys spent fifteen minutes trying to get the Morton home. The line was constantly busy!

"I hope it's Chet calling his mother," Frank said.

But when he finally reached Mrs. Morton, he

was disappointed. Their pal had not returned home and the family had not heard from him. They, in turn, were disappointed that the Hardys had not seen Chet, and Mrs. Morton declared that she was going to communicate with Chief Collig at once.

When the conversation ended, Frank turned to Joe. "What do you think we should do? Keep hunting for Chet, or go on to the shack?"

"Let's go on," Joe replied. "Chief Collig will do everything possible, and we might pick up a clue to Chet's whereabouts by keeping our date."

Frank agreed. They bought two bars of chocolate from the old man who ran the store, then went outside. As they approached their convertible, Joe gasped and grabbed Frank's arm.

"Oh, no!" he cried out, pointing to the two rear tires. Both were flat!

The brothers rushed over to the car. Not only were the tires flat, but to their dismay there were huge slashes in them!

"Someone deliberately cut our tires!" Joe exclaimed.

Frank's face turned white with anger. "Now, what do we do?" he exclaimed.

It was evident that whoever had done the mischief had come there quietly. The boys did not recall hearing a car go past. They wondered whether the tire slashing had been the malicious mischief of some prankster, or whether one of their enemies was pursuing them and doing everything possible to keep the boys from meeting Gorman.

"We have only one spare," Joe remarked with a groan. "Where can we get a second?"

"Maybe the storekeeper sells tires," suggested Frank, and returned to the shop.

Fortunately, the old man kept a few seconds in his cellar. Frank found one that fit the car and brought it upstairs. The kindly shopkeeper, feeling sorry for the boys and disturbed at what had happened, sold the tire to them cheap. Working together, the brothers soon replaced the slashed tires.

"It's way after two o'clock," Frank remarked, as they went to wash their hands. "I wonder if Gorman will wait."

Joe reminded his brother that the stranger might not be at the shack at all. He still mistrusted the man and was sure a trap had been laid for the Hardys.

"Maybe," said Frank. "Anyway, we'll approach with caution."

Two miles farther on they reached a side road which they figured would take them near the shack. It was a sandy, single-lane drive which twisted through the scrub pines. In places it was so narrow that the rain-soaked branches brushed against the side of the car.

Presently the road ended and Frank braked the

convertible to a stop. Ahead of them was nothing but sand. The boys got out and looked around. The wind was blowing a gale and in the distance they could see towering waves, flecked with white caps. They walked closer to the water.

"There's the shack!" Frank pointed to their right, as he put the car keys in his pocket.

The ramshackle old building, badly weathered and sagging, stood between two dunes. The boys trudged toward it through the wet sand, a fine spray from the wind-swept sea stinging their faces.

"What a dismal place!" Frank exclaimed.

Joe smiled grimly. "Perfect spot for a trap!" he muttered.

"I don't believe Gorman's here," Frank said as the boys pushed on, their hearts pounding with excitement. "There's not a footprint leading to the place!"

As they approached the shack, the boys were amazed to see that the front door was wide open. They concluded no one could be inside, for certainly any occupants would have closed the door against the terrific wind.

Nevertheless, Frank cried out lustily, *"Collado!"*

The boys stood outside, waiting for an answer. The countersign which Gorman had suggested was not given, nor did anyone appear.

"It's apparent Gorman's not here," said Joe.

"And if this is a trap, we're not going to walk into it. Let's go!"

At that moment the boys heard a muffled cry from inside the shack. Someone must be in trouble!

Their minds intent on helping the person, the Hardys forgot that they had planned to be cautious. Without a moment's hesitation, the boys rushed into the building.

The next instant they were seized by two masked men!

CHAPTER XVIII

Mixed Identities

AMBUSHED by the two masked men, Frank and Joe fought like wildcats. The assailants were much heavier in build and held the boys with grips of steel. Neither man relaxed his viselike hold for a moment, despite a hard, occasional punch which the Hardys managed to land.

As the boys fought desperately, the face masks slipped off the men. They were strangers to the Hardys.

Joe wrested his right arm free and sent a vicious punch to his adversary's jaw. The man's grip relaxed and he fell back, groggy. Joe's chance for escape had arrived!

"Here I come, Frank!" he yelled.

But in the same instant a kick from the other desperado sent Joe sprawling. In a flash his own antagonist was on top of him. There was little punch left in him but he depended on his great weight to hold the boy down. With the man sitting on his chest and holding his arms, Joe could hardly breathe.

At this point Frank was giving his opponent a rough time. The man was now gasping for breath. "I'll get him really winded," the boy thought, wriggling even harder to break loose.

"Hold still or I'll finish you for good!" the man threatened.

"Just try it," Frank grunted defiantly.

He gave another violent twist and almost broke loose. But the man retained his powerful hold. An unexpected downward swipe with his stiffened hand caught Frank on the back of the neck and the youth slumped to the floor.

The man turned his attention to Joe and helped his pal pin the young sleuth to the floor. He bound and gagged him, then trussed up Frank and tied a handkerchief across his mouth. The men held a whispered consultation, then one of them went into a back room. He returned a moment later dragging something in a burlap sack. He slid it into a corner and both men left the shack by the front door. The boys heard a muffled groan.

A human being was in the sack!

The Hardys concluded it must be Gorman. He, too, had been ambushed! Were the attackers enemies of Gorman working on their own or were they in league with Bowden? Or perhaps Latsky?

Desperately, the boys tried to loosen their bonds. Frank found that by wriggling his jaw and rubbing the gag against his shoulder he could loosen it. At once he cried out:

"Gorman!"

As the bundle in the corner moved feebly in reply, both boys were horrified to see their assailants rush back into the shack. They had heard Frank's outcry. Without a moment's hesitation, they knocked both boys unconscious.

Some time later Joe revived. He was amazed to find that he was outdoors and dusk was coming on. He saw Frank not far away and on the other side of him the person in the burlap sack.

"We're in a gully," Joe thought, as he struggled to rise.

His arms were still tied behind him and the gag was in his mouth. Every part of his body ached. He was lying face up in a puddle of rain water and was soaked.

Frank, still unconscious, was also bound and gagged. His position was precarious; he lay in a deeper part of the ditch with rushing water only inches from his nose and mouth. The stream, swollen by the heavy rain, was tumbling along in torrents.

"Frank will drown!" Joe thought in horror. "I must get him out of here!" He struggled desperately and finally by twisting and turning slipped his own gag off. But his bonds held firmly.

"Frank!" he shouted. "Sit up! Sit up! You'll drown!"

At first there was no response, then his brother made a feeble effort to rise. Frank raised his head a few inches and tried to pull himself up, but he lacked the strength. Exhausted, he slumped back into an even more dangerous position.

"I must rescue him!" Joe told himself.

He dragged his body through the mud to Frank. Rolling onto his side, he was able to clutch his brother by one leg with his tied hands. Getting a firm hold, he pulled Frank inch by inch from the threatening stream.

It was an agonizing task. The sharp gravel on the edges of the gully scraped Joe's cheeks, but finally Joe brought his brother to a safe spot. He managed to remove the gag, but the knots on Frank's bonds defied him. And Frank could not get his brother's untied.

"We'd better give up," said Joe, "or I may be too late to save Gorman."

"Go ahead," Frank said feebly. His own arms had no feeling in them.

The burlap sack lay only slightly out of water. "Those thugs must have figured on having the three of us drown in the stream. They evidently sent us rolling down the bank, but we didn't go far enough."

Redoubling his efforts, Joe crawled to the burlap sack and attempted to secure a hold similar to the one on his brother. But the embankment here had a slimy, mud surface. With each attempt to haul the sack away from the water, Joe lost ground. His own body, instead of catching on the scratchy gravel to give him traction, slipped backward.

"I'll never get Gorman out this way!" Joe groaned. "I'll have to get my hands free."

The bonds were as tight as ever. Joe decided to crawl back to Frank and have him work on the knots again. Halfway to his goal, he heard the sound of an approaching car. Apparently there was a road above the gully!

"Help! Help!" Joe cried out.

The car went by and the boy's heart sank. He yelled even louder. Then, to his immense relief, he heard the car slow down. Then it stopped.

A door slammed, and Joe continued his cries for help. Someone came running and a man leaned over the rim of the gully.

Bowden!

"Joe Hardy!" the man cried out. "Good night. What happened to you?"

"Come down here, quick!" Joe yelled, "and untie me! And we must get the others out!"

Bowden, his raincoat flapping in the wind, grabbed the overhanging branch of a nearby tree for support, and slid down the embankment.

"There's a penknife in my pocket," Joe told Bowden. "Get it out and cut me loose."

"Frank!" he shouted. "Sit up! You'll drown!"

Bowden did so, and together he and Joe freed Frank and assisted him to his feet.

The burlap sack began to move. Bowden jumped back, startled. "For Pete's sake, what's in there?"

"It's—" Joe started to say, when Frank gave his brother a warning look.

"We don't know," Frank spoke up, "but we figure it's probably a man. Two thugs knocked Joe and me out. They must have put all three of us in the gully."

He and Joe made their way to the sack. Both were thinking the same thing. What was Bowden's reaction going to be when he and Gorman faced each other?

With the penknife Joe slashed the cords that bound the burlap sack and yanked it open. A cry of astonishment burst from the Hardys. *The prisoner was not Gorman! He was Chet Morton!*

The stout boy, bound and gagged, and wearing only bathing trunks, gazed at his rescuers stupidly. It was evident he was weak and in a state of shock.

"Chet!" the Hardys exclaimed, removing his bonds.

As their pal took in great draughts of fresh air, Bowden asked, "Is he a friend of yours?"

"Yes," Joe replied. "We must get him home at once."

"I'll take you there," Bowden offered.

"Thanks. Where are we, anyway?" Frank asked him, slapping and swinging his arms to restore the circulation.

"On the shore road about ten miles from Bayport. Say, where did you fellows get slugged?"

"Somewhere up on the dunes," Frank replied offhandedly. He felt in his pocket. "The car keys are gone. I suppose those guys stole our bus."

Bowden preceded the boys up the steep embankment. Frank and Joe assisted Chet, who could hardly put one foot in front of the other.

"You'll feel better, chum, as soon as we get you something to eat," Joe told him.

Chet gave a half-smile and nodded. "Awful hungry," he admitted.

Out of earshot of Bowden, Frank whispered to Chet, "We thought you were Gorman."

"Yes," said Joe. "That guy double-crossed us." He looked at Frank. "I guess you're ready to admit now that Gorman is a phony!"

CHAPTER XIX

Chet's Kidnap Story

As THE three boys followed Bowden to his car, the man's denunciation of Tim Gorman came back to them. Bowden probably was right, but where did he himself fit into the picture? The Hardys wondered if there were any significance to the fact that he happened to be passing this spot when the boys were in the gully.

"The less we say the better," Frank warned the others.

Reaching the car, Joe got into the front seat, ready to grab the controls should Bowden attempt to drive off the main road and lead them into any more trouble. But the man drove along normally and in silence.

Suddenly Joe cried out, "There's our car parked just ahead!" It had been pulled way over to the side of the road. "Our attackers didn't steal it after all."

Bowden stopped and waited as the Hardys examined the automobile. The keys were in it. No one was inside, the trunk compartment contained only the two damaged tires, some tools, and two pairs of old swim trunks. The motor started at once and purred softly.

"Well, thanks again, Mr. Bowden," said Frank, as the three boys transferred to the convertible. By this time it was almost dusk. "We'll have to show our appreciation to you by working harder than ever to locate the demiculverin."

Just then they were startled by a sound that resembled a low, muffled groan.

Frank looked around quickly. "What was that noise?"

"Just the wind in the trees, I guess," Bowden replied as he waved and drove off.

"Well one thing seems certain," Frank remarked as he pulled out onto the road. "I'm sure that Bowden didn't know anything about the attacks on us."

"Maybe not," said Joe. "On the other hand, those thugs may have been in his employ and he was driving out here to see if they had carried out instructions."

"If you're right," said Frank, "he sure got a surprise. And say, what about Gorman? I guess he didn't come to the shack after all."

"But sent those thugs instead," Joe said.

"Listen, you just said it was Bowden."

"Sure I did. I don't know what's going on. I'm completely baffled. And now, Chet, tell us what happened to you. When were you brought to the shack?"

"Shack? Was I in a shack? To tell you the truth, I don't know where I was."

"Don't you remember hearing me call out to Gorman?" Frank asked.

"No. I was unconscious a long time." Chet paused, looking into space. Then he said, "Here's the story. It all began when I put an ad in the paper."

"For what?" Joe asked.

"Skin-diving equipment. I wanted to buy some secondhand. You know how I like to pick up a bargain."

"Yes, we know," Frank said, smiling. "Get on with your story, Chet."

"Well, this morning a fellow my age came out to the farm to see me."

"By the name of Gil," Frank said. "Iola told us when we stopped to see you. What was his last name?"

"Gosh, I don't know. I didn't ask him," Chet said. "I was too excited."

"You mean about getting the skin-diving equipment?" Joe asked.

"That's right. You see, he told me he represented a man who was willing to sell his equipment cheap."

"What happened then?"

"I was out at our pool when he arrived. His car was parked down the road and he offered to drive me to the man's house to look at the gear. Since he was in a hurry, I hopped in without waiting to change."

"What then?" Frank asked.

"This fellow was a crazy driver, believe me," Chet went on. "He was off like a drag racer. On the highway we missed a car by inches as we came into a sharp turn."

The Hardys looked at each other and whistled. "So you were the one in that car that nearly hit us!" Frank exclaimed.

Chet gulped. "It all happened so fast I didn't have time to see who was in the car. My gosh, what if we had crashed!"

"Where did this Gil go then?" Frank prodded.

Chet related that the boy had finally stopped the car in a wooded section which he said led to the house. "As soon as I stepped out, a stocky, masked man jumped from behind a tree. In a flash he had me tied up and blindfolded."

"Then what?" Frank asked.

"While I was lying there in the rain, he said, 'What did you do with the cutlass?' "

"Which cutlass?" I asked. "And fellows, what do you think he did? Kicked me and said, 'You know which cutlass I mean.'

"I told him that I had been to an antique shop

to buy one but had arrived too late. The man didn't have any left. I sure didn't want to tell him about the one you fellows have."

"I'm glad you didn't," said Joe. "Chet, we were at that shop and heard the story. We think the fellow who bought all the cutlasses was Latsky."

"Honest? Good night! That sure complicates things."

"Why did you go to the shop?" Frank asked.

Chet smiled wanly. "I was hoping to get a clue for you fellows on the cutlass Gorman and Bowden know about."

"Good try," said Joe. "Go on with your story."

Chet scowled angrily at the recollection. "When I wouldn't tell that guy anything, he flew into a rage. I don't know what he hit me with but he sure kayoed me. From that time on I don't remember a thing until you found me in the gully."

Just then the car reached the side road which led to the shack where Frank and Joe had been ambushed. Frank turned into it.

"Hey, where you heading?" Chet asked. "I thought you were going to get me something to eat. I'm weak."

"Ten minutes won't make any difference," Frank replied. "I just had an idea."

"Well, it had better be good," Chet grunted.

Frank said it was possible that the figure in the burlap sack at the shack had not been Chet. Why

would his attackers have bothered to take him
there and carry him off again?

"The prisoner was probably someone else—
maybe even Gorman," Frank declared, "and he
may still be there."

"So we're about to make a rescue," Joe spoke
up. "But I'll bet you the person is not Gorman."

"Listen, f-fellows," Chet quavered, "I d-don't
want to be c-captured again."

"You won't," said Frank. "You'll take the car
key and hide in the trunk compartment. You can
act as lookout and give us the old owl whistle if
anyone approaches."

Frank parked in the same spot as before. The
brothers put flashlights in their pockets and got
out. The area ahead was in semidarkness, with the
shack standing out like a black block silhouetted
against the sky.

Frank and Joe moved cautiously, taking care
not to step in the footprints that came away from
the shack. Mingled with them were drag marks,
no doubt made by the feet of the Hardys as the
unconscious boys were removed from the building.

"You take the front of the shack, Joe, I'll go
around back," Frank suggested, as the boys approached it.

The brothers separated. Finding no sign of an
occupant, they finally beamed their flashlights
through the windows. The shack was empty.

In swinging his flashlight back, Joe became aware of something interesting in the sand a few feet away. Quickly he summoned his brother and pointed out a depression in the damp sand.

"Someone was lying there," he said, "face down."

"Well, it wasn't Chet," Frank surmised. "Or Bowden or Latsky." From head to toe the length was a good six feet.

"Look!" Joe exclaimed. "There's an initial here!"

The boys bent over a spot a few inches from the face mark in the sand. Scratched faintly was a letter.

"It looks like a *C*," Joe commented.

"Or perhaps a *G*," Frank said. "It could stand for Gorman."

The boys assumed that the man, bound and gagged, had made the impression with the tip of his nose. A more careful search of the area on the beach side of the shack revealed footprints and drag marks that indicated he had first been taken into the shack, probably in a sack, then later pulled down to the beach and carried off by boat.

The boys trudged back to the shack and again looked at the impression of a face in the sand. Frank felt sure it belonged to Gorman.

"I wish there were some way to make sure," Joe said.

"I think there is," Frank replied, looking down. "Let's make a mold of this face."

The Hardys often made plaster molds of footprints and handprints. They kept the equipment for doing this in their workshop over the garage.

"We'll have to come back and do it later," Frank said. "In the meantime, we'll protect this impression in the sand."

He went inside the shack and looked about for something to use. In one corner was an old box. Carrying it outside, he placed the box firmly over the sand impression so that the wind would not disturb it.

"Let's go!" Joe urged.

As they started back across the sand toward their car, the stillness was suddenly shattered by the mournful hoot of an owl. Chet's signal that something had gone wrong.

The Hardys broke into a run!

CHAPTER XX

An Impostor

THE hooting was not repeated and the brothers wondered if Chet were in trouble. They doubled their speed and quickly reached the convertible. No one was in sight.

Joe pulled up the lid of the trunk compartment which was open an inch. Chet, inside, looked relieved.

"Did you hoot?" Joe asked him.

"I sure did. A couple of guys were here. I heard them coming through the woods, so I gave the signal."

"Where are they now?" Frank demanded.

"Both of them ran back through the woods when they saw you coming."

"Who were they?"

Chet said he did not know. It was too dark to see them well, but neither was the man who had knocked him out. From Chet's description the Hardys concluded they might be the men who had attacked them in the shack.

"They didn't use any names," said Chet, "but they talked a lot." He added that upon seeing the car, they had seemed worried, wondering how it got there. "They decided that perhaps the police had brought it as a decoy. Just then they saw you coming and beat it." Chet laughed softly as he climbed out of the trunk compartment. "I guess they thought you were the cops!"

"It's a good thing they did," said Frank, "or we might have had another battle on our hands."

As the three boys drove home, Chet was very quiet. Joe teased him about it. "So weak from hunger you can't talk?" he asked.

"I'm worried, fellows," Chet said. "I wasn't going to tell you, but maybe I should."

"What's bothering you?"

"When our attackers find out we're still alive, they're really going to make it tough for us!"

Frank declared they could not make it much tougher, but agreed all of them should be on the watch for trouble.

Chet gave a gigantic sneeze. "Those guys'll kill us one way or another," he complained. "But I'll probably die of pneumonia."

Joe wrapped a blanket from the rear seat around Chet's shoulders, but he continued to sneeze all the way to the farm. By the time they pulled into the Morton driveway he was having chills.

"Sorry," said Frank, his conscience bothering him a bit that they had not brought their pal home sooner.

"Look!" Joe exclaimed as they pulled up behind a police car. "Chief Collig's here now."

Mrs. Morton and Iola were overjoyed to see that Chet was safe. Callie, who was spending the night, and the officer expressed their relief also.

Chet's mother at once insisted that he take a hot shower and go to bed. She prepared a light supper, topped off with steaming lemonade.

In the meantime, the police chief, along with Callie and Iola, listened in amazement as Frank and Joe related their experiences.

Chief Collig agreed with the Hardys that the case had assumed serious proportions. "Take it easy, fellows," he advised. "I'll notify the state police about that shack. I'm sure they'll want to station a man there."

"Joe and I plan to make a plaster cast of an impression we found in the sand by the shack," Frank told him. "We thought it might be a good clue."

"I doubt that it will work," said the chief. "But good luck. When do you plan to do it?"

"Very early tomorrow morning."

"I'll tell state police headquarters."

The chief said he himself would put more men

on the case and station a plain-clothes man near Chet's farm. As he left the house, Mrs. Morton bustled into the living room to report that Chet had finally stopped sneezing. "He'll be asleep in a few minutes," she said.

Before Frank and Joe left they telephoned their home. Mrs. Hardy answered and was happy to hear that the boys had suffered no ill effects from their experiences that day.

When they arrived at the house, Aunt Gertrude greeted them at the back door with rapid-fire words of advice about staying away from mysterious shacks.

"We might never have seen you again!" she told her nephews. "I've read about gangsters putting victims into barrels of concrete and throwing them into the sea."

"Ugh!" said Joe, then added with a grin, "That sure would be concrete evidence against them, wouldn't you say, Aunty?"

"Oh, tush!" she said, and went to the stove to remove a panful of warm milk, which she poured into glasses for the boys. "When you've finished this and the supper your mother has prepared, go to bed and get a good night's sleep."

"I guess we'd better," said Joe. "Frank and I have a date at six tomorrow morning." He told her what it was.

Both Aunt Gertrude and Mrs. Hardy sighed, and the boys' mother said, "I suppose it won't be dangerous for you to go if a state policeman is there."

"I'll call you," Aunt Gertrude offered.

Next morning at five-thirty she roused her nephews. "Hurry!" she commanded. "Breakfast is ready and cold eggs and toast are no good."

The brothers dressed quickly and went downstairs to find that their mother and aunt had prepared hot cereal, scrambled eggs, and cocoa.

"The sooner you solve this mystery, the better!" Aunt Gertrude said. "It has me on pins and needles."

"Too bad," said Joe. "But I think we'll be closer to a solution when we make this death mask."

"What are you saying? Goodness! Oh, dear! I didn't know someone was—"

The brothers laughed and calmed their aunt's fears. Then, becoming serious, Frank said he hoped the person whose face had made the impression in the sand was still alive.

Joe, pushing back his chair, said, "I'll carry the equipment from our lab, Frank, while you get the car out."

Shortly after six o'clock the boys started off, promising to report back home by lunchtime.

"I shan't be here," said Aunt Gertrude. "I'm going over to the state museum to a lecture. While there I'll explain about the cutlasses. The trip will take me until ten tonight."

"Happy landing, Aunty!" Joe said, smiling.

It was a pleasant ride in the fresh morning air and the sun stood bright over the horizon when the boys arrived at the dunes. At once they were challenged by a state trooper who stepped from the woods. Frank showed his driver's license and introduced his brother. The man gave his name as Williams.

"Chief Collig said you might come," the officer told them. "Go ahead. There's another officer, named Winn, at the shack."

Lugging the equipment for making the mold, the Hardys trekked across the sand and introduced themselves to State Trooper Winn. He said no one had been there since he had come on duty.

The box was still in place over the imprint of the face in the sand. Joe lifted it. The impression was intact.

"You fellows had a good idea," Trooper Winn remarked. He watched intently as the boys worked.

First, Frank used a spray gun and covered the impression with a quick-hardening fluid. While he was doing this, Joe mixed the plaster in a pail. Then he carefully poured it into the sand.

"When that sets, I hope we'll have a replica of the face, clear enough to be recognizable," Frank remarked.

While waiting for the plaster to harden, the

boys talked to the state trooper about their experience the day before.

"You were lucky to come out of it alive," he said.

When the mold was hard, Frank lifted it from the sand and turned it over. The result was an indistinct blob. Only the chin line was clear.

"Tough luck," the trooper said. "The sand dried out too much during the night."

"Still I'm certain it's Gorman!" Frank said, pointing out the solid, jutting jaw. "He's a victim of those phonies!"

Quickly Joe explained the circumstances to the trooper. "He was attacked by thugs working for higher-ups," he stated.

"Will you tell all this to Williams?" the officer requested. "He'll send out an alarm over the radiophone in his car."

"Let's go!" Frank urged.

The brothers gathered their implements and hurried back to the car. Frank told Trooper Williams of their discovery and he notified state police headquarters from his car, well hidden in the woods, to start a search for Gorman. When he finished speaking, Williams let Frank use the radiophone to contact Chief Collig. The officer said he would institute a local search at once for Gorman.

"I'll let you know if we have any luck, Frank," the chief promised.

Frank joined his brother, then the Hardys said good-by to the trooper.

"What say we stop at Chet's?" Joe proposed as they reached the main road.

"Good idea. I'd like to know how he is. And he'll want to hear the result of our experiment."

They found Chet in bed. There was no doubt he had a cold, but fortunately there was no sign of pneumonia.

"Maybe it pays to be fat," he said, smiling. "Keeps the cold out."

The Hardys stayed with him an hour and brought him up to date on their morning's activities.

"Golly," Chet exclaimed, "where do you suppose Gorman is?"

Frank shrugged. "A prisoner some place of either Bowden or Latsky. I hope the police find him soon. It may solve a lot of problems."

Joe, eager to continue his own sleuthing, arose and said, "Take it easy, Chet. We'll let you know if anything new turns up."

It was noon when the brothers reached home. Mrs. Hardy had a delicious luncheon ready and suggested afterward that they rest awhile. But the boys were eager to continue their search for the demiculverin.

"I'd like to stay out on the dunes until it's too dark to dig," said Joe. "Let's take some supper with us."

Frank agreed. They kissed Mrs. Hardy and said they should be back by nine. Working in the damp sand proved to be a hot, arduous task and just before they ate, the brothers went swimming. When the sun was about to set, they packed their tools and left.

"Not one clue to that demiculverin," said Joe in disgust.

"But we're not giving up!" Frank declared.

Exactly at nine o'clock the Hardys' car hummed up Elm Street and Frank turned into their driveway. The boys noticed a dark-blue sedan parked in front of their home.

"A caller," Joe said. "I wonder who it is."

Pulling up in front of their garage door, the boys got out and went in through the kitchen entrance.

Mrs. Hardy greeted them. "You boys just missed a friend."

"Who was it?" Frank asked.

"Tony Prito's cousin Ken," Mrs. Hardy stated. "He came for the cutlass, as you requested."

"What!" Frank cried in alarm.

Mrs. Hardy explained that when the stranger had come to the door, he had told her that Frank and Joe had been at Tony's house telling about the cutlass. "Tony phoned and said his cousin would pick it up in a few minutes," Mrs. Hardy concluded, "so I wrapped the cutlass in newspaper and gave it to him."

"Mother!" Joe cried out. "That man was an impostor! We weren't there and Tony has no cousin Ken!"

Mrs. Hardy sank into a chair. "Oh, boys, how dreadful!" she wailed. "I'm so ashamed!"

Frank put an arm around her. "Don't worry. But I guess we'd better find that man, Joe."

The brothers dashed to their convertible and sped after the thief.

"There he goes!" Joe cried as Frank turned the next corner.

The convertible leaped ahead. Five blocks farther on, the driver of the blue sedan, apparently unaware that he was being followed, stopped for a red light. Frank and Joe quickly pulled alongside on his left. The man at the wheel wore a black motorcycle jacket.

"Latsky!" the brothers exclaimed.

On the seat alongside him Joe saw a narrow, newspaper-wrapped package. The stolen cutlass!

As Joe flung open the door and hopped out, the man turned to look at the boys. His swarthy face twisted into an ugly sneer.

"We've got you, Latsky!" Joe cried out, quickly reaching for the door handle.

But the ex-convict was quicker. Gunning his motor, he shot across the street against the red light. Joe was flung to the pavement.

CHAPTER XXI

The Wreck

BRAKES screeched as oncoming cars tried to avoid colliding with Latsky. Joe picked himself up and jumped into the convertible. Frank, gritting his teeth impatiently, waited for the signal to change. When it clicked to green, he took off in hot pursuit of the fleeing sedan.

"I hope Latsky sticks to the main highways," Joe said, peering ahead for a glimpse of the fugitive. "With his head start, we'll have a tough time catching him if he turns into a side street."

Reaching the outskirts of the older section of Bayport, Frank increased his speed. Suddenly, going over a small rise, the boys saw the red glow of rear lights. A car swung to the left into a T-intersection highway that circled wide to the right, by-passing the outlying residential section.

"It's Latsky!" Joe shouted.

At almost the same moment, the boys heard the

wailing of a siren close behind them. As Frank made the turn, Joe glanced back.

"A police car," he said. "I guess the officer thinks we're speeding. Slow down, Frank."

The boy eased his foot off the accelerator and the squad car pulled alongside. Chief Collig himself was at the wheel. "Where's the fire, boys?" he asked with a grin.

"We're after Latsky," Frank explained, and quickly told of their chase.

"I'll lead the way!" the chief said, and raced off, the Hardys following.

Though the officer drove a special high-powered police car, Joe doubted that he could catch the fleeing car. Latsky had too much of a head start. "Frank," he suggested, "how about taking the short cut past the old Pell farm? Maybe we could cut back onto the main highway and throw up a roadblock."

"Great! I'll try it."

Frank whirled to the right at the next lane, roared over a narrow macadam road for a mile, and then turned left into another dirt lane. Minutes later he zoomed onto the main highway again.

"Here he comes!" Joe cried out, as two headlights flashed over a low hill behind them. In the distance the whine of the police siren sounded.

Frank slammed on his brakes and angled the convertible across the road, so that the red taillights blinked a warning to stop. Both boys jumped out, concealing themselves behind a tree along the roadside.

"Wow!" Joe whispered. "Latsky and the chief must be doing ninety!"

The next second there was a squeal of rubber on concrete. Latsky had spotted the roadblock and jammed on the brakes. His car swayed from side to side.

"He's out of control!" Frank cried, as the oncoming car headed wildly for the tree behind which the brothers had taken cover.

As the boys ran, the car caromed off the tree, screeched across the road into a field, where it overturned.

"Whew!" Joe gave a low whistle as he and Frank sped toward the wreck, flashlights in hand.

While they were still some distance from it, they saw Latsky, carrying the cutlass, stumble from the car. Dazed for the moment, the man staggered, but quickly regained his equilibrium and dashed off into the darkness of a woods beyond.

At that moment Chief Collig roared up and stopped. Seeing the flashlights, he got out and hurried across the field. The Hardys were trying to pick up Latsky's footprints.

"Am I seeing things?" the officer cried out. "How did you get here? And what's going on?"

"Short cut," Joe said. "We set up a roadblock

and stopped Latsky, but he ran into these woods."

Swinging the bright beams of their lights in the woods, the trio of pursuers followed the footprints. They led to a wide brook.

"Latsky's clever," Chief Collig remarked. "He must have entered the water and walked either up- or downstream."

The brothers offered to take one direction while Chief Collig took the other.

The officer shook his head. "No use. I'll radio from my car and have the place surrounded."

The three left the woods. While Chief Collig went ahead to phone from his car, the Hardys paused to look over the wreck of Latsky's car.

"He dropped the cutlass!" Joe cried out excitedly as his flashlight picked up the glint of the shining steel blade.

Grabbing it, he hurried with Frank to the police car. Chief Collig was just concluding his conversation. The officer said he was delighted to hear that the boys had retrieved their ancient sword, then said, "My men are starting out now to track down Latsky. By the way, that wrecked car was stolen. Too bad."

Soon a tow truck arrived to haul the smashed sedan back to the police garage. The Hardys said good-by to the chief, and with the cutlass in their possession, started home to give it a close examination.

After telling their mother and Aunt Gertrude,

who had returned, that they had retrieved the weapon, Frank and Joe went directly to their laboratory over the garage. Switching on the powerful work lamp, they quickly examined the blade. On one side was etched the name of the maker, *Montoya*.

"There's probably more," said Joe excitedly, getting out bottles of chemicals with which to clean off the metal. Every inch of the fine Damascus steel blade was inspected for other markings or hidden writings. There were none.

"The maker of this cutlass must have considered it too fine to mark," Joe said. Old as it was, the sword still had a keen edge.

Next, the handle was cleaned. Every seed pearl in the design was intact, and the gold leaf was still in place.

"Let's examine that handle closely," Frank suggested, getting a magnifying glass.

There was a heavy, richly encrusted leaf scroll pattern. The Hardys scrutinized this minutely to see if it concealed any gems or contraband. Until almost midnight they continued the inspection, but without success.

"I still think there might be something in this handle," Frank said stubbornly. "Let's try that special magnifying glass of Dad's."

"Good idea!" said Joe. "I'll get it."

He ran back to the house and in a few minutes returned with the extra-powerful glass.

Frank focused it over the handle inch by inch. Suddenly his face lighted up. "Look here, Joe!" he exclaimed.

Following Frank's finger, Joe saw a tiny line which had been cleverly worked into the leaf pattern. "Do you think it's an opening?" he asked.

"Yes."

With the thin blade of a knife, Frank tried to force open the crack, but this proved impossible.

"Maybe there's a spring hidden somewhere in the handle," Joe suggested. "Let me try it."

Frank handed the cutlass to him and Joe bent over it intently. He pressed each tiny leaf with no success. The crack did not widen.

"Maybe it has some connection with the blade," Frank mused. "But how?"

"The spring could be rusted after all these years. I'll try hitting it on something," Joe said.

He looked around the laboratory and found a slab of stone left over from a previous experiment. Grasping the handle of the cutlass firmly, he jabbed the tip against the hard surface.

Click! The crack widened a full inch!

The boys were jubilant. Frank knelt and quickly but gently picked up the sword.

"The tip contains a tiny mechanism," he said after a moment's scrutiny. "It extends through the blade all the way to the handle."

He inspected the opening and reached into it with his thumb and forefinger.

"Anything there?" Joe asked, holding his breath.

Frank nodded. Gingerly he pulled out a piece of ancient parchment.

"There's writing on it!" Joe exclaimed.

Frank smoothed out the parchment so the boys could read it.

CHAPTER XXII

Gunner's Tools

"FRANK, this message is written in a foreign language," Joe said, disappointed that he could not read it.

The words were not in modern Spanish, but the boys thought they might be an old version of the language.

"Whatever it says must be mighty important," Frank concluded, "or the writer wouldn't have hidden the message."

"And Bowden and Gorman and Latsky must think so too," Joe added. He grinned. "Frank, we beat 'em all!"

Happy but weary, the boys went to bed, the cutlass safely tucked under Frank's mattress.

At breakfast the next morning they showed the old parchment to their mother and Aunt Gertrude. All were bending over it excitedly when Chet walked in.

"Wow!" he said when he heard the newest development in the mystery. "You boys sure are good detectives."

"We're not good enough to read this," Frank admitted. "We must find someone to translate it right away."

At that moment the phone rang. "I'll take it," Joe offered, hoping the caller would be Mr. Hardy.

The other boys followed him to the phone and stood near as he spoke.

"This is Joe," he replied to the speaker. The caller spoke for some time. Placing his hand over the mouthpiece, Joe whispered to Chet and Frank, "Come here. It's Bowden!"

He held the receiver a distance from his ear to let the others hear the conversation. Bowden said that Gorman had just been arrested in St. Louis while traveling under an assumed name.

"Good night!" Joe exclaimed, then asked Bowden how he had received this information.

"A friend of mine on the St. Louis police force, knowing I was interested, just phoned me," Bowden replied. "I guess we can go about our job of locating the cannon without any further interruption from fakes like Gorman."

The boys were skeptical of the story. It certainly did not ring true.

To Bowden, Joe merely said, "Thank you for the information. We're working hard on the case."

The man told Joe he would let the Hardys know if anything further developed. He was about to hang up when Chet burst out:

"Tell him we've found the clue in the cutlass!"

Frank gave Chet a warning look, but too late. Bowden's next words were, "I heard what someone just said. Congratulations, Joe!"

Before the boy could make any comment, Bowden went on to say that he had planned to tell the Hardys of the cutlass clue, which he had heard about several months ago.

"I had a feeling, though," he said, "that it might be just an old rumor, so I kept the story to myself. And besides, I figured that being such clever detectives, you and your brother would discover the truth, anyway."

"I see," replied Joe noncommittally. Then he said good-by and hung up.

Chet apologized for revealing the news about the cutlass. The brothers were disturbed but assured him that by working fast they would get to the bottom of the mystery and no harm would result from Chet's slip.

"Now if we only could think of someone who might translate the message on the parchment," Frank said thoughtfully.

"Let's try our Spanish teacher, Miss Kelly," Joe suggested. "If she—"

At this moment the doorbell rang. Aunt Gertrude went to answer it and was given a telegram.

"It's for you boys," she said, handing over the message to Frank.

"This wire is from Dad!" the boy said, as he unfolded the message. "Say, Joe, it's in code!"

The brothers dashed up to their father's study and removed Mr. Hardy's code book from his filing cabinet. Quickly they unscrambled the message. Their jaws dropped as they read:

BEWARE DOUBLE-CROSSING OF BOWDEN!

"Double-crossing!" Frank echoed the warning in the telegram. "Dad must have further information about Bowden."

"I wish he had told us more," Joe said, as the brothers returned to the first floor with the news of Mr. Hardy's message. Instantly their mother and Aunt Gertrude became alarmed.

"After all that has happened," said their aunt firmly, "I think you should leave town for a while. You can take me on a trip in the car."

The boys were fearful they might be forced into making the trip. Both instantly promised to take extra precautions from now on.

"If Bowden still doesn't suspect that we mistrust him," Frank said, "we'll have the advantage."

"Which we hope to hold until Dad returns," Joe added.

Chet whistled. "Well, count me out of any more trouble," he said. "I'm off for home. Let me know what that foreign parchment says, will you?"

After Chet had chugged off in his jalopy, Frank suggested that they call on Miss Kelly and see about having the parchment translated.

"Let's stop at police headquarters on the way," Joe said. "We'll check Bowden's story about Gorman's arrest."

With the parchment tucked securely in Frank's inner pocket, they drove to the police station. There the sergeant in charge promised to check with the St. Louis police about the alleged arrest of Gorman. Before leaving, Frank asked if the man named Guiness who had exploded the fireworks had been caught. The officer shook his head.

"Please let us know what you find out about Gorman," Joe said as they walked out.

Frank drove across Bayport to the small cottage where Miss Kelly lived. She was a pleasant, middle-aged woman, well liked by her students.

"We wondered if you could help us solve a mystery," Joe said, as they all sat down in her cool, attractive living room.

"By the expressions on your faces I thought you must be working on one," Miss Kelly said. "What is it?"

Frank produced the parchment. "Is this Spanish, and can you translate it? The words have us stumped."

The teacher studied the scrawled writing for a

moment. "No wonder," she said. "This is written in Portuguese—old-fashioned Portuguese at that."

"What does it say?" Frank asked eagerly.

"I'm sorry, but I can't translate it," the woman said slowly. "But I think a Mrs. Vasquez I know might help you."

Handing back the parchment, Miss Kelly explained that Mrs. Vasquez was an elderly Portuguese woman, the mother of a fishing boat captain.

"Mrs. Vasquez isn't well and doesn't get up until afternoon," Miss Kelly explained, "but I'm sure if you went to see her after lunch, she would help you. I'll give you her address." She looked in the telephone directory and wrote it down. The boys thanked her and left.

"If we can't get the message translated until after lunch," Joe urged, "let's go out to Pirates' Hill and call on Sergeant Tilton. Maybe he can give us some idea of where to dig."

"Okay," Frank agreed. "We haven't had any luck ourselves." He drove out to the sand dunes.

The boys went directly to Tilton's cottage. Dressed in dungarees and a coonskin cap, the sergeant was working in his small flower garden.

"He probably doesn't have buckskins to match the hat!" Joe whispered.

The man was in high spirits. "Hi there, boys!" he yelled.

"Good morning, Sergeant," Frank replied.

"We've come to do some more digging for that cannon."

"I see."

"We thought maybe you could show us where you think it should be," Joe added.

"Well, now, let me see," the man drawled as he came toward them. "Suppose I walk around the place with you." He grabbed up a folding canvas chair.

When they had gone about fifty yards along the dunes, he stopped and scratched his head. "Accordin' to my system of reckonin', the gun must have been located just about— No." He moved a few steps to his left. "Just about here."

While Sergeant Tilton lighted an old pipe and seated himself comfortably on his folding chair, the boys started digging. The ex-gunner told them story after story of his Army adventures while they spaded deep through the white sand.

"Hold everything!" Joe called some time later. He was standing waist-deep in a hole. "I've found something!"

He bent over and came up with a queer-looking gadget. "What would this be?" he asked, handing it to the sergeant.

Tilton examined it carefully. "This here's a gunner's scraper!" he replied.

"Probably belonged to the same gear as that primer Chet found the other day," Frank whispered to Joe.

Protected by the sand, the scraper had withstood the ravages of time better than the primer had.

"The cannon's just *got* to be near here!" Joe declared excitedly.

"That's right, my boy." The sergeant wore a knowing look as he handed the scraper back to Joe. The man resumed puffing on his pipe. "Don't stop diggin', lads." He blew out a small cloud of smoke.

Ten minutes later Frank spaded loose a six-foot-long wooden pole fixed at one end with an iron blade. As he handed it to Tilton, the old ordnance man exclaimed, "It's a handspike! You must be gettin' close!"

CHAPTER XXIII

Guarding a Discovery

THOUGH eager to dig quickly, Frank and Joe paused a moment to stare at the strange-looking pole.

"What was that used for?" Frank asked Sergeant Tilton.

"To manhandle the heavy cannon," he replied. "With this tool, the gunners could move the carriage, or lift the breech of the gun, so's they could adjust the elevatin' screw."

"Boy! We're getting hot!" Joe exclaimed triumphantly. "The cannon will be our next find!"

Jubilantly expectant, the Hardys dug deeper into the sand. But nothing further came to light.

Finally Frank straightened up with a sigh. "Joe," he said, "it's noon. We'd better let our search go for now. You know we have an errand in town."

Joe had almost forgotten their plan to call on

Mrs. Vasquez and have the parchment translated. "You're right, Frank." He asked Sergeant Tilton to keep the spike and pole until the boys called for them. Then the brothers quickly refilled the hole, took their tools, and started back to town.

After stopping at a diner for a quick lunch, the Hardys drove directly to the dock area, where they easily found Mrs. Vasquez's modest home. Her daughter-in-law answered their knock, and when Frank explained the boys' mission, they were ushered inside.

A white-haired old lady with black eyes stared curiously at the Hardys from a rocking chair. She smiled, adjusted her black shawl, and motioned for them to be seated.

"Mother doesn't speak much English," the daughter-in-law said, "but I'll translate your conversation."

The Vasquezes spoke rapidly in Portuguese, then the old lady leaned back in her rocking chair and read the parchment. When she looked up, more words in Portuguese followed between the women.

"What is she saying?" Joe asked eagerly.

"Mama says this message gives directions."

"For what?" Frank's heart pounded with excitement.

Again there was a rapid exchange of words in the foreign tongue, then the younger woman smiled. "Directions to a cannon. Is that right?"

"Wow! I'll say it is!" Joe could not contain himself. "Frank, this breaks the case wide open!"

The older boy remained calm. He asked, "Does it say where the cannon is located?"

"Yes. I'll write it all down."

"In English, please!" Joe requested.

As Mrs. Vasquez spoke, the younger woman translated and wrote:

On high rock Alaqua Cove due east setting sun first day July is treasure cannon. Demiculverin.

The woman smiled. "Does this mean anything to you boys? Where is Alaqua Cove?"

"That was the old Indian name for Bayport, I think," Frank replied. "Thanks a million. And please, will you keep this a secret—for a while at least."

"Oh, yes, Mama and I will say nothing until you tell us we can. I'm glad we could help you."

Frank and Joe bowed to Mrs. Vasquez, then left the house and drove off. They were grinning ecstatically.

"At last we're going to solve this mystery!" Joe exclaimed jubilantly.

"The time of year is perfect," Frank said. "If we goof this time we'd better go out of the detective business."

"Right."

On reaching Pirates' Hill with their digging

tools, Joe became uneasy. "I hate to wait until sunset. Can't we start?"

"Sure. I've been here so much the past few days I can tell you exactly where the sun will set." Frank pointed to a distant church spire. "Right there." He took a compass from his pocket and moved about until his back was due east of the spire. "The cannon should be somewhere along this line." He shuffled through the sand.

"The directions said 'high rock,'" Joe reminded him. "There are rocks under this sand. Let's try the highest point on this line you've made."

The boys set to work. For half an hour they dug furiously. Finally, Frank's spade struck metal!

"J-Joe!" Frank exclaimed. "This must be the cannon!"

A moment later they uncovered the curve of a barrel, and judging from its dimensions, they were convinced that this was the Spanish demi-culverin for which they had been searching.

"Success!" Joe cried, thumping his brother on the back.

Frank wore the broadest grin his brother had ever seen. "This is super!" he exclaimed.

The two boys began to dance a sailor's hornpipe. Then suddenly Frank sobered. "We'd better be careful!" he said. "Someone might be spying on us!"

"Joe! This must be the cannon!"

"You're right," Joe agreed. "We'd better cover the gun up again."

With their shovels the boys quickly concealed the valuable discovery until they could come back the next day and uncover it completely. Then, to bewilder any prying eyes, the Hardys decided to make small excavations at other spots. They wandered off and started to dig here and there.

A short time later two figures appeared over the dunes. Chet and Tony Prito!

"We came out in the *Napoli*," Tony said. "Figured you might be here. We called your house. Your mother said if we found you fellows to give you a message."

"About Gorman," Chet added. "The police left word that he's not in St. Louis."

"Just as we suspected," said Frank. "I wonder if Chief Collig has any news about Gorman."

"No," said Chet. "He phoned there was no progress on that score. Say, have you fellows had any luck out here?"

Frank, in a low voice, told about finding the demiculverin. "Yee-ow!" Chet exploded.

Tony congratulated his friends and asked what the Hardys' next move would be.

"We'll dig up the whole cannon tomorrow," Frank replied.

"I sure wish we could stay here tonight and get an early start," Joe said. "Say, why don't we all camp out for the night and stand guard over the cannon?"

"Swell idea," said Frank. "Remember Dad's warning about Bowden—he may double-cross us. And that could happen any minute."

Tony offered to go back to town and pick up a tent, sleeping bags, and food. "I'll call your folks and tell 'em, fellows," he promised.

The camp on Pirates' Hill was in readiness by nightfall, with the tent pitched on the cannon site. As the stars came out, the Hardys and Chet crawled into their shelter. Tony had volunteered to stand guard first and posted himself outside the tent flap.

At ten o'clock Tony became aware of an approaching figure. Instantly he awoke his sleeping pals. They waited tensely until the person was almost at the tent.

"I'll get him!" Joe cried.

The campers lunged out of the shelter and Joe was about to tackle the oncoming figure when they recognized him.

"Sergeant Tilton!" Frank exclaimed.

The boys smiled at the man's clothes. He looked enough like a pirate to be one!

"So it's you," drawled the elderly man. Sergeant Tilton explained that he had spotted their flashlights and come to see who his new neighbors were. "I was just tryin' on this outfit from my pirate collection when I saw the light."

Knowing that the old man was inclined to gossip, the boys decided to keep secret their finding of the cannon. They chatted casually with Tilton, telling him they had set up camp to be ready for some sleuthing early in the morning.

"Well, boys," the sergeant said finally, "I reckon I'd better git back to my shack. I suspect you'll all be snorin' soon." He chuckled and walked off.

The rest of the night passed quietly, with the boys rotating the watches as they had planned earlier. By six o'clock they were up and preparing breakfast. After eating, Frank, Joe, and Tony started work under the tent, with Chet acting as lookout.

Within an hour the three boys had dug a deep pit and uncovered the entire demiculverin. The old fieldpiece appeared to be in good condition.

"What a beauty!" Frank exclaimed.

"And look at this number on it!" Joe cried out. On the barrel were cut the numerals 8–4–20. "It must be a code for this type. Let's find out what it stands for."

Leaving Chet and Tony on guard, the Hardys went home in the convertible to check through their father's books on cannons. Joe's hunch that the numerals might be a code led to nothing. They read on.

Suddenly Frank exclaimed, "I get it! An eight-pound ball and four pounds of powder."

"And twenty degrees of elevation!" Joe beamed.

Hearing the excited talk of the boys, Mrs. Hardy looked into the room and asked, "Have you found out something interesting?"

"Sunken treasure!" Joe exulted. "A ball shot from the demiculverin probably marks the spot where the old merchantman was sunk by the pirates in that Battle of Bayport!"

Mrs. Hardy was astounded. She started to praise her sons when the front doorbell rang. Frank hurried down to answer it. Opening the door, he blinked in amazement.

Bowden!

As Frank recovered from his surprise, he said, "Come in," and called loudly over his shoulder, "Joe! Mr. Bowden's here!"

Joe came down the stairs like a streak of lightning. "What was up now?" he wondered.

Bowden smiled. "Can't stay but a few minutes. Good news travels fast. I understand you've located the cannon I asked you to find!"

The Hardys were dumfounded. They stared speechlessly.

"I'll have the money for you shortly for solving my case," Bowden continued. "And I'll send a truck out to the dunes tomorrow to pick up the demiculverin."

. . . demiculverin . . .

CHAPTER XXIV

Human Targets

THOUGH looks of dismay showed on the Hardy
boys' faces, they did not affirm Bowden's statement that they had located the demiculverin.
Neither did they deny it.

"Where did you hear we found a cannon?"
Frank asked.

The man's reply proved to be another bombshell. "I was out there and your friends told me."

Frank and Joe were too astonished to make an
immediate comment. They exchanged quick
glances, each coming to the same decision. Whatever Bowden's real reason was for wanting the
ancient cannon, they were going to try keeping
it from him until further word arrived from their
father or the police.

Bowden smiled. "I now own Pirates' Hill."

As the boys watched, thunderstruck, he took

192

several impressive-looking documents from his pocket and showed them to the boys. One was a certificate of sale, another a government release, and the third a letter with a notary-public seal. This stated that Bowden had a right to anything found on Pirates' Hill.

"They certainly look authentic," Frank said, but realized the papers could be clever forgeries.

Mr. Hardy's dire warning to his sons indicated that Bowden was probably a confidence man. It was highly possible that he had accomplices who could imitate signatures and even print fake documents.

Suddenly an idea came to Frank. The stock certificates of the Copper Slope Mining Company which Bowden had sold to Mr. Ash in Taylorville might be counterfeit!

"I must get in touch with Dad about this," Frank concluded.

He and Joe knew that the only course to pursue right now was not to let Bowden become suspicious that they suspected him! This thought was telegraphed from one to the other, but Joe winced a bit as his brother spoke.

"It looks as if the hill is yours all right, Mr. Bowden. If there's a cannon on it, there may be other treasures, too."

Frank's assurance pleased Bowden. "I hope you're right. And I'm glad you boys see the whole thing my way. To tell you the truth, I thought you might want the old cannon yourself. Accept my congratulations for a grand job!"

After he left, Frank went into a huddle with his brother and told him about the possibility of the stock being counterfeit. Joe whistled and suggested that they compose a telegram in code to their father telling him this, and mentioning the fact that the cannon had been found and Bowden was claiming it. Frank phoned the message to the telegraph office.

"I hope this information will bring Dad up here," Joe said. "Frank, this fellow is crooked. We can't just hand him the cannon!"

"Of course not. Don't forget, Joe, digging out the sand around the demiculverin so it can be lifted, and lugging the two tons of iron over the sand will be no child's play. It may take days. Maybe something will happen in the meantime to stop Bowden."

"Let's hope so," said Joe. "Well, what say we do some computing on those numbers we found on the cannon?"

He felt that they would indicate where a ball would land if it was shot from the cannon when the gun barrel was raised to the 20 degrees of elevation. The brothers quickly discovered that they were unable to solve the gunnery problem exactly.

Frank suggested that they drive over to see Mr. Rowe, head of the mathematics department at

Bayport High School. "He's teaching summer school, and I'm sure he'll be there now."

The boys set off for Bayport High and found that fortunately Mr. Rowe was having a free period. Intrigued by the problem, he went to work, filling several sheets of paper with calculations. At last he said:

"The cannon ball would land two thousand yards away, if trained and elevated at precisely the angle given in the figures."

Frank and Joe thanked the teacher, then hurried to their car. On the way back to the dunes, Frank remarked that if the demiculverin had not been moved from the position in which the pirates had placed it, and currents had not shifted the ship, the ball should land exactly on the spot where the sunken merchantman rested. "And that's where the treasure will be!"

"If your guess is right," Joe said, "we could get permission from the Coast Guard to fire one ball, locate the spot, and then hand over the cannon to Bowden—with our compliments!"

Frank grinned, but reminded his brother that whatever their plans, they must work fast. "Bowden is not going to let any beach grass grow under his feet!" he warned.

Driving directly to Pirates' Hill, they parked off the shore road as before and ran up the dune to rejoin Chet and Tony.

At the edge of it Joe stopped short. Grabbing

Frank by the arm, he cried out, "Well, look over there! Bowden again! We can't lose him!"

At the site of the cannon, he and Sergeant Tilton were talking to Chet and Tony.

"Good-by to our little plan," Joe said woefully.

"Maybe not," Frank remarked hopefully as they rushed forward.

Chet and Tony dashed up to meet the Hardys and whispered that after Frank and Joe had gone back to town the boys had continued digging. The two men had caught them off guard.

"You can see the cannon very plainly now," Tony said. "Chet and I thought we'd surprise you and dig out all the sand from the front of it."

Frank quickly related Bowden's visit to the house. Tony frowned. "Maybe that gossipy Sergeant Tilton told him we were here. They might even be in league!"

As the group reached the men, the Hardys received only a nod from Bowden, but the genial old sergeant began to talk excitedly. Today he was resplendent in the blue field uniform of a Northern officer of the Civil War. He explained that at Bowden's request he was preparing a charge similar to the one he used to test the mortar in the town square at Bayport.

In spite of Bowden's efforts to signal him to keep quiet, Sergeant Tilton continued, "An' I'm goin' to test the strength o' the barrel fer Mr.

Bowden. He wants to be sure it'll be safe fer him to fire off durin' that there Exposition in Floridy."

At once the Hardys were suspicious. "Are you sure you aren't planning to shoot a cannon ball off right now?" Joe asked.

The old gunner looked in disgust at the boy. "Of course not. That'd be against the law. I'd have to git permission from the Coast Guard."

"That's right," said Joe, eying Bowden to watch his reaction. But the man showed none.

As the boys watched Sergeant Tilton, he prepared the powder charge and fired the gun. A thunderous boom followed. As the smoke cleared, he rushed back to inspect the piece for the presence of any cracks.

"She stood up fine!" he exclaimed. "First rate!"

"Well, thanks, Sergeant," said Bowden. "I guess the cannon will do for the pageant. I'll see you later," he added as he walked away toward the road.

The old man began running his hands along the cannon and talking to himself. "Great piece o' work," he declared. He turned to Frank and Joe. "I'd like to tell you a bit about this."

"We'd like to hear it a little later," said Frank.

The Hardys were eager to try locating the old sunken merchantman. When their friends agreed to help, Frank asked Chet to drive to their boathouse in the convertible and pick up the aqualung diving gear. Tony offered the use of the *Napoli* from which to work.

When Chet reached the road where the Hardys' convertible was parked, Bowden was just driving away. As the car gathered speed Chet saw a piece of paper blow out the window. Picking it up, he examined it curiously.

"Why, it's a stock certificate of the Copper Slope Mining Company!" he said to himself. "It must be valuable. I'd better return it to Mr. Bowden."

Then a thought struck him. "This was the stock Frank and Joe were talking about. It might be phony!"

At once Chet decided to leave the certificate at the Hardys' home for inspection later on. He got into the convertible and drove back to Bayport.

Out on the dunes, Frank was just saying to the old sergeant, "Tell us about this cannon."

Tilton beamed. "Firing a gun like this here one is a pretty risky thing."

He went on to explain that the demiculverin most likely had been used at some Spanish colonial fort before the pirates had captured it. The normal life of such a cannon was twelve hundred rounds. But in the outpost, where it was hard to get new weapons, a piece like this was always fired many rounds beyond that figure, increasing the danger of explosion with each burst.

"When cracks develop 'round the vent or in the bore," Tilton said, "you got to be mighty careful. The muzzle sometimes blows clean off 'em!"

Digging away more sand, the boys found that the cannon was mounted on a mahogany four-wheeled truck carriage used on all eighteenth-century ships and garrison guns. It was covered with beautiful leaf designs, wrought in iron.

"Look!" Joe cried. "It's chained to a boulder."

This convinced the Hardys that they had been right in their deductions. The cannon was placed so that a ball fired from it would strike one particular place in the ocean!

The boys took sights along the gun barrel and checked them with their compass. The barrel pointed due east. This would make it easy to estimate the approximate spot where the treasure should be. They chafed under the necessity of awaiting Chet's return.

"What you fellows aimin' to do, now that you got this mystery solved?" Tilton asked them.

"Look for another case, I guess," Joe replied. "Right now we're going for a swim." To himself he added, "And look for the buried treasure!"

"Hm," said Tilton. "I ain't been in the water fer nigh onto thirty years."

He climbed off the gun emplacement just as Chet came hurrying across the sand. He was not carrying the diving gear.

"Something's up!" Joe declared.

Puffing, Chet halted in front of the others. "I've got big news. Chief Collig phoned your home, Frank and Joe. Latsky's been captured!"

"Honestly?" Frank exclaimed, hardly daring to believe it was true.

"Great!" Joe cried out. "How?"

"Latsky finally returned to the cabin. Seems he had money buried there and had run out of funds," Chet replied. "The police had no trouble nabbing him."

Joe grinned. "Latsky'll be back in his old cell for a long stretch."

After a brief discussion about him, Frank looked at Chet. "In all the excitement I guess you forgot our diving gear."

Chet laughed and told him it was in the car. The four boys said good-by to Tilton and went to pick up the gear. On the way Chet told the others about the stock certificate Bowden had dropped and that Mrs. Hardy now had it.

"Swell work, Chet!" Frank thumped his friend on the back.

The diving equipment was carried to the beach. As the boys waded out to the *Napoli,* Joe reviewed what they would do. Tony and Chet were to remain aboard the boat, while Frank and Joe did the diving.

"We'll work by dead reckoning on the first attempt," Joe told his pals. "Frank and I will go over the side at the estimated distance from shore."

"Let's get started," Tony urged.

"Hold on!" Frank said. "I think we're foolish to leave the cannon unguarded with Bowden loose. No telling what he may try to pull."

"What do you suggest?" Joe asked.

"That one of us go back and watch. If Bowden comes, our guard can signal and we'll get to the hill in a hurry."

"I'll do it," Chet offered. "But how can I signal you?"

Tony took a large yellow bandanna and a clean white rag out of the boat's locker. He handed them to Chet. "Wigwag with these," he said.

"And be sure to hide behind a dune," Frank cautioned, "so Bowden won't see you."

"Gee, I'm really going to be busy," said Chet, as he sloshed back through the water.

The others climbed into the motorboat and Tony started the engine. Frank and Joe gave directions to the site of the sunken treasure, using the church spire as a landmark and keeping on a course due east. Tony steered the *Napoli* carefully while Frank and Joe tried to estimate a distance of two thousand yards from shore.

"Stop!" Frank commanded presently. "Unless all our reckoning is wrong, the treasure ship must be directly below us."

There was silence for a few moments as the

full import of the boy's words struck them all. They might be about to make an intriguing find!

"Let's go down!" Joe urged his brother.

The Hardys donned their gear and climbed over the side.

Tony, watching Chet intently, suddenly cried out, "Wait, fellows! Chet is signaling!"

Back on Pirates' Hill their pal had seen Bowden sneaking up to the cannon. As he watched the man, terror struck his heart. Bowden was ramming a charge of powder into the ancient gun. Then he inserted a cannon ball into the muzzle!

All this time Chet was wigwagging. The boys on the water interpreted, *"Bowden here. Look out for—"*

The missile ready, Bowden ran to the back of the cannon and inserted a fuse into the vent hole. Chet's hands were shaking with fright. Bowden flicked on his lighter and held it to the fuse, then stepped back.

"Run!" Chet signaled.

Boom!

With a shuddering detonation the demiculverin sent the deadly ball directly toward the *Napoli!*

CHAPTER XXV

Divers' Reward

WHAM! *Smack!*

The cannon ball hit the *Napoli* full force a second after the three boys had flung themselves away from it. Spray and debris flew in every direction.

The Hardys, only a few feet away, were knocked unconscious by the concussion. Tony, unhurt, was worried about his companions. He realized that in their diving equipment they would float and could breathe even if they were unconscious. However, he was afraid that his friends might not have survived the shock.

Catching up to Joe, he was just in time to see the boy move his arms. He was alive!

"Thank goodness!" Tony said to himself.

He told Joe a cannon ball had been fired at them and advised him to dive deep to escape a possible second shot. The boy nodded.

Tony went to find Frank. To his relief, he too had regained consciousness. Tony overtook him.

"Better go deep," he warned. "Another cannon ball may be fired at us!"

Frank lifted his mask. "How about you?"

"Never mind me."

"I'm sticking," said Frank simply. "Anyway, if Tilton was right, the cannon might have blown up."

"Do you think Bowden meant to kill us?" Tony asked.

"It certainly looks that way."

Just then Joe surfaced and the three boys looked at the *Napoli*. One glance told them that it was doomed.

"Too bad," said Frank.

"Yes," Joe agreed. "Guess we'll have to swim to shore. Stick close to us, Tony."

The boys struck out toward the distant beach, but they had not swum fifty yards when they heard the roar of a motor launch.

"A Coast Guard boat!" Joe called out.

The launch circled once, then pulled in closer to pick them up. The young lieutenant in charge, who introduced himself as Ted Newgate, was glad to hear that the boys were all right. He glanced at the ruined *Napoli*.

"We heard two reports of a cannon and came to investigate," he said as the boys were hauled aboard. "What's going on here?"

"Someone on the hill tried to blow us out of the water," Joe answered. "I want to get to shore as fast as possible and find him."

The powerful marine motor kicked up white foam as the boat headed toward land. Nearing Pirates' Hill, Frank gave a startled cry. "Joe, there's Dad!"

"Where?"

"Over there on the beach with Chief Collig and Chet."

Joe shaded his eyes. "And look who's hand-cuffed to Collig! Bowden!"

Quickly the boys told the lieutenant about the secret of Pirates' Hill. The young man was amazed and congratulated them on their good work. Then he cut the motor and put them ashore in the launch's gig. When the bow hit the sand, Frank and Joe hopped out and raced across the beach to greet their father, a handsome, strapping man in his early forties.

"Are you both all right?" he asked.

"We're okay, Dad, but no thanks to Bow-den," Frank replied.

The police chief said, "You boys can thank your lucky stars you're still here to tell the story. The charge against Bowden will be assault and battery with intent to kill. And the Coast Guard will have something to say about his firing with-out permission."

Bowden looked completely beaten. The police

chief explained that the man had stolen a cannon ball from the town square the night before, hoping to put it to use some day and locate the site of the sunken merchantman.

"When he spotted you fellows out there, Bowden saw a good chance to eliminate you from the race for the treasure."

Joe glared at the prisoner. "We didn't trust you from the start, but we didn't think you were a killer."

The police chief said Bowden had brought about his own arrest. "If the repercussion from that old cannon hadn't knocked him out, he would have got away before your dad and I showed up. He was armed, so Chet wouldn't have had a chance to stop him. Well, greed will catch up with a guy sooner or later. Bowden will have a long stretch in prison to think this over."

Frank asked his father how he happened to have come to Pirates' Hill. "Because I hoped Bowden was here and I wanted to have him arrested at once for selling fake stock certificates." Mr. Hardy smiled broadly at his two sons. "You've helped me solve my own case of bringing a notorious gang of swindlers to justice. I've been tracking this fellow's friends all over the South. His real name is Layng. They've been counterfeiting legitimate types of stock, getting prospects through the mail and selling them phony certificates."

Chief Collig beamed. "I hear you fellows kept playing Bowden along like a hooked marlin!"

Joe inquired when Mr. Hardy had arrived from Florida. "Only an hour ago," the detective said. "When your telegram arrived, I came up here in a jet police plane. Chet clinched matters by leaving the stock certificate he picked up when Bowden dropped it. The instant your mother handed it to me I recognized it as a counterfeit."

Hearing this, the prisoner winced, chagrined to think that he had given himself away by carelessly losing the certificate.

Collig started to walk toward the shore road. "We'd better get this man Bowden behind bars," he said.

The others followed. When they reached the police car, Chief Collig phoned headquarters to report he had a prisoner. In turn the sergeant on duty reported that he was holding a suspect for the Hardy boys to identify.

"Follow me in your car," the chief told Frank and Joe, "and we'll find out who it is."

On their arrival at police headquarters, the brothers were first shown a black skin-diving suit and a yellow-trimmed skull cap by the sergeant.

"Good night!" Joe cried out. "The guy that nearly winged us wore gear like this. Where'd you get it, Sergeant?"

"From that man over there. His name is Guiness."

The Hardys turned to look. "The man who shot the rockets at us Fourth of July!" Frank exclaimed. "Say, Guiness," he said, walking over to him, "how did you know we were going to be there that night?"

"I didn't," the prisoner answered, "but my chance came right then and I took it."

Guiness admitted he was in league with Latsky, whom he had met recently. But the prisoner denied knowing Bowden or anyone named Gorman.

"What about the paper with the name Smedick on it which the police found in your wastebasket?" Frank asked. "Didn't you know Smedick was Gorman?"

Guiness denied this, saying Latsky must have discovered Gorman's alias and dropped the paper on one of his visits to Guiness's room.

"Where is Gorman?" Frank shot at Bowden.

He did not answer, but this fact gave Frank a lead. As events flashed through his mind, an idea came to him.

"You had Gorman attacked back of the shack on the beach and taken away in the boat he had rented to get there. Later, you hid him in the trunk compartment of your car. We heard him moan."

Bowden's face went ashen. Frank's surmise had turned the trick. Bowden confessed that he had lied to the boys about Gorman's character. He had had him trailed and ambushed at the shack by henchmen. When the Hardys arrived unexpectedly, it had been necessary for the thugs to attack them too. Worried, they had taken the Hardys to the gully and dumped them. Then they had abandoned the car.

Coming back to the shack they had met Bowden and told the story. Later, Bowden had driven past the gully to check and received a real surprise.

"I had to rescue you because I wanted you to think I was on the level," Bowden said. "That moan you heard in my car was Gorman. I told you it had been made by the wind."

"What about him? Where is he?" Frank persisted.

"Gorman's in good shape," Bowden said. "You'll find him in the room next to mine at the motel, tied up. He's supposed to be sick and has an attendant. No one else goes in."

Chief Collig said he would send two men there at once to release Gorman and bring him to headquarters. While the others waited, more facts came out about the case.

During a prison term, Bowden had met Latsky who knew a lot about ancient cannon, including the story of the Battle of Bayport. Each man determined to find the treasure for himself after being released. It became a bitter race between the ex-convicts, with Gorman against both of them.

"First you had to locate the cutlass with the directions," said Frank.

"Yes," Bowden admitted. "Latsky tried to get the old cutlasses from the Bayport Historical Society building but failed. Then I took them."

Joe snapped his fingers and said, "I see how it went. When you found none of them contained the parchment, you had Gil Fanning sell them for you. Latsky later purchased the five cutlasses only to find that none of them contained the parchment."

"Yes," said Frank, "and you had Chet lured off to be questioned and slugged and put in the gully with Joe and me."

As he was talking, two officers walked in with Gorman and an eighteen-year-old youth.

Chet gazed in amazement. "That's the fellow who got me in trouble!" the stout boy shouted, doubling up his fists.

"Take it easy," Chief Collig advised. "I'll handle this."

The new prisoner was introduced as Gil Fanning, Gorman's attendant. He said he was a newcomer to Bayport. His parents had died and he was now living with his grandparents. He had needed money, so he had started working for Bowden.

"I—I didn't think I was doing anything wrong," Gil said. "Then first thing I knew, I was in so deep I couldn't get out. It'll kill the old folks when they find out."

Bowden admitted that the boy had been his dupe, and hoped that harsh punishment would not be meted out to him. The ex-convict at first would not reveal the names of his henchmen, but finally he did, and Chief Collig ordered their immediate arrest.

The Hardys turned to Gorman and asked if he felt all right. "Yes," he said, "and I'm glad you fellows uncovered the secret in the cutlass, instead of Latsky and the others."

He told them that the directions to the location of the cannon, according to the legend, had been hidden in the cutlass belonging to the pirates' captain. It had been lost ashore during a scuffle among the pirates themselves.

"Go on! Go on!" Joe urged as Gorman paused.

The former Navy man said he had learned about the treasure and the demiculverin from an ancient diary. "It was written by the wife of the merchantman's captain," he said. "She tried for years to locate the site of her husband's sunken ship."

Gorman said he was a direct descendant of the captain and had the diary in his possession. After an honorable discharge from the Navy he had decided to try finding the sunken treasure.

"Which I never could have done if you boys hadn't found the cannon, and Mr. Hardy and the chief hadn't caught Bowden," Gorman said.

Joe smiled and asked a question of Bowden. "Was it Latsky who threatened you in the message we found on your door and sent us one?"

Bowden nodded. "He later knocked me out when I was talking to you fellows on the phone."

"And tell me, who was hiding under the tarpaulin in the boat when Halpen warned us away from the sting ray?"

"I was," Guiness replied. "I told Halpen to give you that phony story. And Latsky hired me to dive for the sunken treasure ship. When you boys showed up while I was at work, I thought you were hunting too. So I shot at you with a spear to scare you off."

Joe whistled. "When I saw that spear coming, I had no idea that Frank and I would be involved in an undersea treasure hunt.

When the questioning ended, the prisoners were led away and the others left. Mr. Hardy invited Gorman to stay at their home until he had recovered completely from the manhandling he had received.

"Thank you. I accept," the young man said, smiling.

"And please forgive Joe and me for suspecting you," Frank spoke up.

"I will on one condition," Gorman replied

with a grin. "That you four boys show me where that treasure is and let me share with you whatever the government will let us take."

The Hardys laughed and Joe said, "That won't be hard to take!"

"But first," said Frank, "from whatever we get, I suggest that we buy Tony a new and even better *Napoli.*"

The others quickly agreed, then Joe said, "I guess this treasure hunt will be the most exciting adventure we've ever had."

But another was soon to come their way, which was to become known as **THE GHOST AT SKELETON ROCK.**

Two days later the whole group, in skin-diving outfits, climbed over the side of the *Sleuth* and descended to a depth of thirty feet. There lay the ancient merchantman, its timbers rotted away, and moss and barnacles covering the metal parts.

Cautiously Gorman and the boys swam in and out, removing the debris. At last their search was rewarded. There, in the uncovered hold of the old vessel, lay a vast quantity of gold bullion. Through their masks, the divers beamed at one another triumphantly.

The Hardys and their friends had found the ancient treasure!